Dying Freedom

Dying Freedom

Insurrection 1810

Rubén Acosta Vallejo

Copyright © 2011, 2013 by Rubén Acosta Vallejo.

Library of Congress Control Number:		2013911516
ISBN:	Hardcover	978-1-4633-6071-9
	Softcover	978-1-4633-6070-2
	Ebook	978-1-4633-6069-6

All rights reserved. No part of this book may be reproduced or transmitted in any form or by any means, electronic or mechanical, including photocopying, recording, or by any information storage and retrieval system, without permission in writing from the copyright owner.

This is a work of fiction. All of the characters, names, incidents, organizations, and dialogue in this novel are either the products of the author's imagination or are used fictitiously.

This book was printed in the United States of America.

Rev. date: 28/10/2013

To order additional copies of this book, contact:
Palibrio LLC
1663 Liberty Drive
Suite 200
Bloomington, IN 47403
Toll Free from the U.S.A 877.407.5847
Toll Free from Mexico 01.800.288.2243
Toll Free from Spain 900.866.949
From other International locations +1.812.671.9757
Fax: 01.812.355.1576
orders@palibrio.com

Praise for "Dying Freedom"

"This saga brings many literary elements together and is not only informative but also entertaining. The history is as tantalizing as the romance."
      Perry Baxter, Literacy Coach

"A fantastic story about love, loyalty, and independence. You won't be able to put it down and you'll want to read it again and again."
      Suzy Flores-Muñoz, Educator

"Readers will travel back in history close and personal. A real education. A strong candidate for a motion picture."
      George A. V. Villalobos, Movie & TV Production

"Dying Freedom" is a sweeping historical novel of love and redemption during the most significant time of the Mexican Independence war. A book to be read and re-read. A book with a compelling story written with luminous simplicity and power."
      Paul Paniagua MA, Literature

"Dying Freedom brilliantly takes you back in history in a timeless story of love and social justice. World leaders and parents should reflect on this book's universal truths and poetic justice."
      Arnulfo AV. Moreno, Educator

"I wish we would read a story like this one in my English class."
      Aileen Ruby, High School Student

Historical fiction with a timeless romance. Be prepared to embark on an educational journey to Mexico's past.
    Alicia Cuellar, Educator

"One of the greatest stories ever told; once you start reading you won't want to stop!"
    Oscar Herrera, Accountant

Acknowledgments

My deepest gratitude to all the people who took time and interest in this work. I am thankful for my wife Ivonne for her consistent support, love, and confidence. To my very first editor and illustrator Aileen, and to Allan my example in effort and discipline. Para Chuy, Bertita, Arnulfo, y el George mis hermanos del alma. Heartfelt thanks to my mother Amparo for her love, sacrifice, and inspiration. Nunca te podría pagar.

I express appreciation to one of my best friends and mentors, a great story teller and talented musician, my grandpa "Papá Toño." He wished for the rising generation to learn about their forefathers.

Special thanks to Dr. Jan Osborn, Artyn Gardner, Suzy Flores-Munoz, Veronica Franco, Angelica Berber-Prado, Perry Baxter, Alicia Cuellar, Pablo Paniagua, Oscar Herrera, Teresa Fisher, Claire Jimeno, Linda Herrera, Jorge and Denise Mendez, and so many friends named and unnamed.

Prologue

The Aztec and Mayan empires had fallen before the Spanish gunpowder and religion for the past 300 years. Tons of gold and silver from the colony had helped to maintain the Spanish Armada as one of the most powerful forces in the world. A share of the wealth had also provided enough means to expand the church in the colonies. The turn of the 19th century seemed promising, but the Creoles were growing in influence and numbers. The Spanish Crown controlled and taxed goods from the New Spain and struggled to regulate all transactions.

Many of the Spaniard Aristocracy had invested and taken the land near the silver mines in the central region of the country. Being a Spanish landholder in the New Spain had advantages because they received all the goods and sold them back to the peasants. They also freely traded amongst themselves. The Mexican natives were cheaply paid and almost forced to labor in the estates or the dark mines. Hacendados were the law within their estate. But now, Napoleon's forces in Northern Spain encouraged the rebellious atmosphere in New Spain.

History and Chronology of the 1810 Insurgent Movement in New Spain

September 13, 1810 - Revolutionary conspiracy and much of the insurgent planning, weapons, and supplies for the beginning of the revolution originally planned for December 8, 1810, was discovered in Queretaro. Josefa Ortiz de Dominguez notifies insurgent leaders.

September 16, 1810 - El Grito de Dolores ("Cry of Dolores") also known as El Grito de la Independencia, was uttered by Miguel Hidalgo y Costilla at the small town of Dolores, near Guanajuato. It is the event that marks the beginning of the Mexican War of Independence.

Around 6:00am on September 16, 1810, Hidalgo ordered the church bells to be rung and gathered his congregation. Accompanied by Ignacio Allende and Juan Aldama, he addressed the people in front of his church, encouraging them to revolt.

September 28, 1810 - Siege of Guanajuato. When Miguel Hidalgo y Costilla's insurgent troops threatened to take over this city during the Mexican War of Independence; Corregidor Reaño secured himself in the Alhóndiga on 28 September 1810, along with many other Spaniards and some rich Creoles. He believed that the strength of the building and its positioning would make it easy to repel the insurgent's attacks. The belief held up at first, but soon the revolutionaries burned down the eastern door and attacked their oppressors. Most of the people hiding in the building, most of them Spanish families from the outskirts of the city, were murdered and the building sacked. At the end of the day, hundreds of people were dead, and the whole city of Guanajuato pillaged. This event encouraged Hidalgo not to attack Mexico City because he was afraid his followers would repeat the massacres and looting of Guanajuato.

Miguel Hidalgo y Costilla – (8 May 1753 – 30 July 1811). A Mexican priest and a leader of the Mexican War of Independence. Hidalgo is called the Father of the Nation. He declared slaves free and slavery illegal in 1810. He was a Creole born in Pénjamo, Guanajuato, Mexico.

Guanajuato - A city and municipality in central Mexico and the capital of the state with the same name. The origin and growth of the city resulted from the discovery of minerals in the mountains surrounding it. The mines were so rich that the city was one the most influential during the colonial period. Guanajuato was also the site of the first battle of the Mexican War of Independence between insurgent and royalist troops at the Alhóndiga de Granaditas. The city was named a World Heritage Site in 1988.

Alhóndiga de Granaditas - An old grain storage building in Guanajuato City, Mexico. This historic building was erected from 1798 to 1809, by orders of Juan Antonio de Reaño y Bárcena, a Spaniard who was the quartermaster of the city during the Viceroyalty of New Spain. The edifice was used for the buying and selling of wheat, corn, and other grains. Prior to the Mexican Independence from Spain, it was used as a warehouse, military barracks, and prison. Currently it serves as a museum. The building received World Heritage listing as part of the Historic Town of Guanajuato in 1988.

Miguel Hidalgo, Ignacio Allende, Juan Aldama, and José Mariano Jiménez - These first insurgent leaders were beheaded in 1811. Their heads were hung from the corners of the Alhóndiga, to discourage other independence movements.

El Pípila - His real name was Juan José de los Reyes Martínez Amaro. Pípila was a miner from the town of San Miguel. When the Spanish barricaded themselves in the grain warehouse known as the Alhóndiga de Granaditas, he was instrumental in breaking into the fortress. Pípila moved with a flat stone tied to his back to protect himself from Spanish troops' bullets. He carried tar and torch to the door and set it on fire.

Creole - (Criollo-Spanish) A person of pure Spanish ancestry born in the Americas during the Spanish American colonies.

Hacienda - An estate or land grant. The hacienda system of colonial Latin America was a system of large land holdings aimed to produce economic revenue for the estate owner. Aside from the small circle of Spaniards and Elite Creoles at the top of the hacienda society, the rest of the people were peasants, or mounted ranch hands variously called vaqueros (cowboys). There was no court of appeals governing the haciendas. Stock raising was central to ranching haciendas. In areas where the hacienda included working mines, as in Mexico and Peru, the patron might be immensely rich.

Hacendado - Also called patron, the owner of a hacienda.

Jaripeo - A competitive event similar to rodeo developed from animal husbandry practices used on the haciendas of old Mexico. It evolved from the traditions brought from Spain in the 16th century. It is also called Charreada.

Table of Contents

Acknowledgments 7
Prologue 9
Chapter 1   Crossing of the River 15
Chapter 2   La Casa Grande 21
Chapter 3   Blacksmith Shop 27
Chapter 4   The Hacienda 37
Chapter 5   First Encounter 46
Chapter 6   Horse Riding 55
Chapter 7   Choosing Destiny 71
Chapter 8   The Prophecy 80
Chapter 9   The Subintendent as Regidor 93
Chapter 10   Jaripeo 124
Chapter 11   Mourn 139
Chapter 12   The Race 146
Chapter 13   Last Dance 152
Chapter 14   Fugitives 165
Chapter 15   Guanajuato 185
Chapter 16   The Alhóndiga 211
Bibliography 219

Crossing of the River

The crow's cry in the dark orange horizon increased the guards' uneasiness. They knew the sunset would beat them to the fort where safety and a warm meal awaited. Three iron stagecoaches with the Spanish Crown imprinted on the right side moved slowly along the dusty road. Major Joaquín Vallejo monitored the transportation of silver from the Guanajuato mines to Mexico City. From there, the precious metal continued its voyage to El Puerto to be shipped to Spain. There were serious risks on the two-week trip, but Vallejo's army was strong and ready to quell any attacks by thieves or insurgents. The company had been down this road several times, but today there was a visible fear on their faces.

The exploited canyon had been left without trees, without signs of the approaching autumn. The dust wrestling with the wind blocked the end of the basin. The travelers should have been at the San Juan Del Rio Fort before dark, but the axle incident put them behind schedule. The fort stored the ammunition and provisions for the army. It was also a secure place to keep the gold and silver overnight. Vallejo knew they would be safe inside the meter thick stonewalls. Having been stationed there as a guard and even as a night watch, he knew the place well.

This time, Joaquin did not worry about crossing the river like previous times. That wasn't the main problem. It was the truth in his chest and the assurance of his soldier's blind trust, which made his thoughts broil.

"My men will support my decision as soon as they learn my motives, but they need to hear the truth from me and no one else. Come on Vallejo control yourself! There is nothing to worry about! But what if they revolt? They will be doing the right thing because they pledged their loyalty to the Crown, but I am digging a pit right in their path! No, no way! They can't be that blind! They are of sound understanding! They will choose liberty and justice!"

Once his soldiers were more relaxed at the fort, the chief officer planned to reveal his crushing secret.

The chilling sound of the trumpet startled the company as Vallejo raised his arm.

"LISTEN! We will arrive at the fort in one hour! Keep alert as we continue through the canyon. Don't stop until we reach the riverside! Blow the whistle if you distinguish any movement in the dark. Sergeant Portillo should be waiting for us on the other side of the river. Have your muskets ready just in case! Is that understood?"

Vallejo looked at his three sergeants each signaling understanding. He motioned for them to make sure the men followed suit. Joaquín was a stern man who punished disloyalty. He was caught in the middle of the dilemma. His career as a soldier made him a Realist, but deep in his heart he questioned his loyalty to Spain. Vallejo sometimes felt he was on the wrong side of justice, especially when he saw the army pushed away the natives when they begged for food.

The scene when he was left for dead in the battlefield played over and over in his mind. It was also the time when he first saw his wife Teachiayotl, the young Indian woman who saved his life.

"I will not fail you! I am doing it for our son Leonardo! I will fight to defend the native's rights; it's time to do it openly. I will show my brother Antonio that he is wrong about us," lamented Joaquin as he remembered his brother's last comment.

"Dealing with the Mexican natives is like dealing with a contagious disease, I will never mingle with savages whose intelligence is only above the dogs."

Such prejudice was only a result of ignorance and a hidden wedge in Antonio's soul. He became obsessed with having more possessions than Joaquin. He assumed that economic stability would come after finishing his studies in Toledo. But poor judgment and heavy drinking frightened away solid opportunities for enterprising. A bitter jealousy cankered his heart every time he heard about his brother's achievements in New Spain. Antonio objected to the rumor of having a mestizo nephew. The very idea made him angry with Joaquin. It had been a great embarrassment to his name and he hated the mocking by the other estate owners in the area. Despite all of Antonio's efforts to hide the truth, the Major admitted that he indeed had a Mexican son—Leonardo, seventeen years old now. Vallejo was mortified by the situation,

"Education and refinement would shield him from ignorance and discrimination. If my son becomes a physician, the way should be open for him."

It was Vallejo's assignment and contract with Vice-Royalty that kept him away from home and delayed his son's education. The Major also knew that the government was about to take a different direction which included violence. It was imperative for Leonardo to leave the country. He would be safe in Europe, but the trip was not paid for yet.

Vallejo had toiled in this area for more than twenty years. His risky commission was well known in Guanajuato and Mexico City. That is why he suffered constant assaults on the post. Such was the perilous life of a soldier who couldn't make it to the rank of a general, but he had been bright enough to recognize opportunity in the New World. Now, he found himself on this weary journey with a frightened company. He had thought about his career the whole day. The guilt in his chest convinced him to make this his last assignment before retirement.

As the armed escort advanced, the sound of the river rapids usually became a soothing chime. Not today, Vallejo's conscience could not hide his covert. The horses' hooves beating on the ground agitated his heartbeat. His eyes were fixed on the trail that seemed to go underwater and continued uninterrupted to the other side of the fifty foot wide current.

"They will fight among them! There will be bloodshed! No, I can't do that! They will consider me a traitor," Joaquin wrestled with his thoughts.

"Sometimes a few good men have to perish to accomplish a greater good. I will risk it all! Enough! I will get this off my chest once and for all when we cross the river!"

Once by the riverbank, Vallejo raised his hand indicating to one of his sergeants to dismount as if preparing to attack. Nobody seemed to be waiting for them on the other side. There was only a small dock with a ferryboat used to get the cargo across the river. The soldiers were ordered to release the horse-drawn carriages, but first, half of the tired army took turns to cool their faces and wash the sweat off. The full moon sparkled in the water like a lighthouse beam. The Major made sure the team of black horses was led across the river first, and then on the second trip, the load would be placed on the ferryboat.

"Come on! We don't have the whole night to cross the river!" he yelled.

Six men pushed the ferry with long poles and four more paddled. The current wasn't strong, and the horses were uneasy in the middle of the water. After reaching shore, two men jumped in the shallow water. They were holding a rope to secure the vessel to a post on the dock. Only four men crossed back, leaving the other six, alert to any surprise attack.

"I will stay with the cargo! Portillo better show his nose right this second! Go and find that crook!" hollered Vallejo as his men hesitated to advance any further, "Never mind, let's bring the cargo across without delay!"

When the ferry returned, he directed the first stagecoach to be placed at the end, making space for the other two. Again, six men pushed with the poles and four more paddled. This time, three soldiers and Joaquin leaned on the sealed rectangular boxes with their muskets ready. Most of the army had yet to cross the river. The Major looked attentively toward the other side because this was the most vulnerable time. At that moment, exactly in the middle of the river, a rain of bullets roared through them. His men began to fall one by one, the vessel carried slowly downstream by the current. At first, he thought his soldiers had betrayed him, but there wasn't anybody on the other side. He crawled under a carriage, but still, he couldn't see the enemy. He was certain it was the revolutionaries. Three of his men had survived the first attack and were shouting to the soldiers who had not crossed the river. There was an exchange of fire from both sides. Major Vallejo was caught in the middle again, second guessing his decision, and aware that his soldiers still didn't know about his pact with rebel forces. Joaquin Vallejo had deviated the cargo destined to Mexico City Realists officials into the hands of General Ignacio Allende's revolutionary army. The firing ceased for a moment before resuming with greater fury. The vessel continued southward now past the dock.

Ropes were thrown to secure it, to pull it across the river. Joaquin tried to take out his pistol, but an intense pain in his back paralyzed him. It was so severe he couldn't breathe. He lay there immobile, under a black cargo stagecoach on a ferry, in the middle of the river. His only hope was to abandon the vessel that was a few feet from shore. He made a last effort and pulled himself to the back of the ferry. He thought of surrendering, but he knew the fate of the chief captain in this situation. Before he slid into the river, he made an attempt to look at his assassins. He was only able to see flashing gunfire right above him. Once in the water, he was carried by the current. He knew it was a sure death because he couldn't swim in his condition, and the river began to pick up speed. Suddenly, he felt some branches and grabbed the end of one. That was his last effort to save his life, and the last thing he remembered about that night.

Three days later, he woke up in Guanajuato surrounded by men. The pain in his back was so brutal that he almost lost consciousness again. In his agony, he recognized his brother Antonio by his side. Joaquin pleaded with him to recognize his Mestizo son Leonardo and to take care of his education. Leonardo's mother, Techiayotl, had died when Leonardo was ten years old. It was Joaquin's wish to bring a private tutor to La Casa Grande and prepare his son for the University in Madrid. Joaquin's will left everything to Leonardo. It included the Vallejo Estate, two hundred acres of land, five hundred head of cattle, fifty horses, and La Casa Grande. There was also a one hundred liter clay jar full of silver coins. They were hidden in a secret chamber by the well, which only Leonardo and Joaquin knew existed.

La Casa Grande

Two weeks later, two men in uniform delivered a telegram to La Casa Grande. Their long faces revealed the bad news. They were commissioned by the Guanajuato Corregidor to offer condolences in the name of the Crown. They refused to enter the premises if Vallejo's son wasn't present. In a moment, Leonardo rushed to the door thinking it was his father's soldiers. He was disappointed when he didn't recognize any of them. His trembling hands opened the envelope and fixed his eyes on the lines. Little by little, the words became swords to his soul. The man whom he thought was the strongest and most intelligent was gone. Shattered were his dreams of travel and conquest. All he ever wanted in life was to please and become like his father, but it was over now. As he stared at the door, his mind went back in time. He saw a little boy who resented his father's long trips. Several times, he had clung to his father's legs and cried into the afternoon after his parting. Today, as a matured teenager, he had to mourn his father's death without any other family member to share his grief.

Even after his brother's death, Antonio resented having a Mestizo nephew. He couldn't contain the disgust. In his mind, he was determined to hide Leonardo's identity to the world. For him, status and power were stronger than blood; therefore, he did everything in his power to obtain his brother's possessions.

Three weeks after the Major's death, Antonio made the trip to Central Mexico. He met with Don Julio Cortez and secretly changed his brother's will. He did not hesitate to secure all assets for himself. Once in La Casa Grande, he asked to speak alone to Leonardo.

"You are going to España tomorrow. I am going to take care of all your needs," he said as he played with the gold chain attached to his watch.

"Who are you? Who sent you here?" asked Leonardo.

"I am in charge of all of your father's business and will make sure you go to Madrid and study there. Maybe someday you will become a soldier for El Rey Fernando. Hurry up and get ready! Don Julio will take you to El Puerto on your way to Madrid."

"My father told me that a teacher from Madrid would come here and continue my instruction. I don't want to leave my house!" protested Leonardo.

"You are going to do exactly what I say! And it is the last time I want to hear you call Joaquin my father!" Do you understand me? You don't have a father, or maybe you do! He might be digging for silver in Guanajuato!" Antonio scolded angrily holding the young man by his arms.

"Help! Esteban! Let me free! Don't you touch me!" cried the young man.

The native servants seeing the heated episode turned around and left the room.

"I am in charge now! In charge of your life!" hollered Antonio, "Be grateful that I have arranged room and board for you with Don Julio Cortez! There is a professor in his house teaching his daughter already. Now, get your baggage and get in the carriage!"

"Why did you say I was going to Spain then?" questioned Leonardo.

"You are not ready for the university yet! The Cortez Family will help you get ready. They will teach you better manners!" barked Antonio.

"I do not want to leave my house! Can't they come and stay here?" Leonardo proposed.

"This is not your house anymore. Everything belongs to the Crown now. Your father was in debt, he owed everything he had. You will be fine with Don Julio, start packing immediately!"

Leonardo prepared his luggage and looked out the window. His watery eyes glanced at the stable where Lightning neighed. It was as if the stallion sensed Leonardo's deep grief and parting. The horse had been a gift from his father, and the young man cared for Lightning like his family. Both grew up in La Casa Grande, and today might be their last day together. Outside, Antonio and Don Julio spoke about business and their intentions to sell the estate.

"I am sorry about your brother. Have you heard who betrayed him? It must have been somebody who knew the route well," Don Julio puzzled, "I know it is not the right time to settle our transactions, but what will you do with the youngster?"

"I don't want to see the savage again! Make sure he never finds out the truth! If he misbehaves, do not hesitate to fix him. A few strikes a day will teach him to obey!"

"Don't you worry my friend, I'll take care of him!" replied Don Julio, "He will learn to work as any other heathen in this, our New Spain."

Leonardo came out and was put in the carriage on his way to the Cieneguilla Estate where Don Julio was the Hacendado. Don Julio's family consisted of his wife, Rosa, and his daughter, Beatriz. He was a keen businessman, his sharp nose and small blue eyes had been trained to smell and see a good opportunity. Don Julio had been in New

Spain for thirty five years. All this time, he was hoping for any enterprise in Guanajuato where the silver mines gave a bigger purse. He was a man of influence but very small means. At one time, his wealth was as big as his eyes could see; five hundred acres of land from Jocucar to Ojo Caliente near El Camino Real. Currently, the colony's economic uncertainty and his ambition had reduced his assets. He only saw one way out of debt, fraud. Like many wealth conquistadors, among his favorite hobbies were horse breaking and racing. But he was getting too old to compete with his neighbors.

As they prepared to leave, the sound of a colt in the corral caught Don Julio's attention.

"What a sweet surprise! Look at that beast! I almost left without it." My daughter has been asking for a white one just like it. Let's see him!" exclaimed Don Julio.

"That's Lightning my horse! Please let me bring him. He is not a trouble maker," Leonardo pleaded. The young man ran into the corral to prepare the stallion for the trip.

"I promised my daughter a horse like that one, but look at that stallion! Just my luck!" laughed Don Julio.

"That beast will bring you trouble. Look at the way it follows the kid! He will run away on the beast!" warned Antonio

"No, no! I will put distance between the two. You go and don't worry about the horse."

"Can I ride Lightning all the way?" Leonardo asked as he came out of the corral.

"Of course not!" bawled Antonio, "You get in the carriage, and let's use the animal to carry some luggage."

The sun was beginning to set when they left La Casa Grande. Leonardo's heart felt heavy as he sobbed quietly. The dusty road impeded a clean, clear last view to the Hacienda from the carriage, but in his trodden mind the impression of home would remain forever. Even Don Julio and Antonio's conversation about politics and economics grew old and left for the night when they fell asleep. Outside, the echo of a coyote's howl joined the owl's vigil song. On the black horizon, the moon looked down with empathy and added a shadow that faithfully followed the carriage and the white colt. The dusty trail resembled a giant snake that slid through hills and valleys and survived the deep cut of the canyons. The mesquite trees appeared to be mute witnesses that had fallen asleep on their watch. Leonardo had more than enough time to plan his escape. All he needed was to get on horseback and fly like the wind, but grief for his father's death and the idea of being an orphan clouded his tired brain.

"You will be fine young man," Don Julio encouraged, "You have to be strong and get on with your life. It is better for you to come and work, I mean, study at my house than to remain a lonely one."

"How long will I stay at your house?" Leonardo asked.

"I am not sure. It all depends on how much you know about science and how fast you learn," Don Julio replied, a little puzzled by the question.

"My daughter Beatriz will board in the University of Toledo next year. She has been taught by a private professor for the past three years. Of course, she is brilliant!"

Leonardo was delighted to hear that. He liked the idea of becoming Beatriz' friend, but Don Julio immediately disliked the look on the young man's face.

"How did my father die?" asked Leonardo.

"He had a very dangerous profession; at this time, things are getting out of hand. Everywhere we go, we hear that Creoles, Mestizos, and even the Indians rebel violently and cause many problems. Look! There is something you have to understand. We have to live in a civilized way and these people do not want to be educated or refined. The Mexicans better choose to live according to the mandates of the Crown, or they will disappear from the land," declared Don Julio, "Joaquín was surprised by thieves who wanted a share of the Crown's wealth. The wounds were so severe; even the best doctor in Guanajuato could not do anything to preserve his life. His biggest concern was you, and we are going to make sure his will is done. I am sorry my young friend!"

"I didn't say good bye. I need to see his grave!" exclaimed Leonardo rubbing his eyes.

"Relax my friend, get some rest, you will be fine," Don Julio said trying to comfort the young man.

"I will not rest until his murderers are brought to justice!" Leonardo called out.

Blacksmith Shop

The next morning when everyone woke up, they were in the outskirts of Teocaltiche. From the distance, the cathedral's towers seemed to pierce the cotton clouds beneath the blue sky. It was a resting place where travelers stopped for wheel repairs and to buy merchandise for their estates. Zenón and his son Mariano were the only blacksmiths in town. They always accommodated Don Julio, since he was their boss. They had known each other for years, and the inn was big enough for the company to lodge. The property was next to an old wheat mill, also owned by Don Julio.

"Buenos dias patrón! Bienvenidos! Breakfast is ready," greeted Mariano, the sixteen year old who served the merchants. His father Zenón was a skinny, overworked blacksmith who depended on Don Julio's meager wages to feed his family. He relied on his son Mariano, his daughter María del Socorro, and his wife San Juana to keep up with the shop and the inn's demands. His other three children were still too small to earn wages. Of course, the Hacendado always took care of the earnings. Don Julio made Zenón accountable for every earned and spent centavo. Mariano was a natural leader, he knew every estate owner who traveled through the growing town. He also had become an expert trader. He knew exactly what Don Julio needed but resented his strong manners and occasional whippings. It was Don Julio's bodyguards who made him think twice about rebelling. As every other young man, he had been beaten and threatened to lose his parents.

"Mariano, have the book ready for me! I want to see this month's expenses!" shouted Don Julio with his mouth full of tortilla.

San Juana made sure the boss' demands were met. That morning, she got up at five to prepare the best meal of the month. She did not know how many people would eat at her table, but she made sure there was enough food for ten. The spicy chilaquiles and chile colorado's aroma didn't help a tiny bit to control her fears.

When he woke up, Leonardo went directly to check on his horse. María Del Socorro directed him to the corral in the back of the shop. There, he gathered a few corn leaves and water for Lightning.

Realizing his charge was not inside; Antonio called out, "Leonardo! Leonardo! Where did you go muchacho? Where is Leonardo?" he shouted to anyone within earshot.

"He is in the corral feeding his horse," replied María Del Socorro. Don Julio and Antonio ran to the back of the house to verify the girl's words.

"He can't go any where. He doesn't know anybody, and besides, we won't lose much if he gets lost anyway!" Don Julio said with a sarcastic tone, "Calm down! As long as the horse is here, he hasn't gone anywhere and look, the horse is here!" he continued trying to calm Antonio.

As they were speaking, the young man came with a bucket full of clean water and took it to the stallion.

"I have found the perfect assignment for Leonardo! He will take care of my horses," commented Don Julio laughing.

"See, there is nothing to worry about!"

For the first time, Antonio paid close attention to the boy. He thought he was seeing his brother Joaquin thirty years earlier.

"Look, this is where we separate. I don't need to worry about an Indian kid who has brought shame to my last name. After breakfast, I am leaving for Guanajuato on my way to Mexico City. I will sell Joaquin's assets and pay you your share," grumbled Antonio annoyed by Leonardo's company.

"You are too dramatic. The kid is a fine young man! He will be useful in my estate. Come on, let's go in and have breakfast," suggested Don Julio.

"Dramatic! You say that I am dramatic! Are you considering the possibility that this Indian is related to me? That is a direct insult to me, my family, and my class! Don't you assume or even bring up this conversation with anyone! I forbid you! Do you understand?" Antonio demanded angrily.

"Pardon me, I take it back. It didn't come out right," Don Julio admitted.

Both men walked back to the kitchen and sat at the table. San Juana had already served breakfast, and Zenón and Mariano were ready to explain all expenses to Don Julio.

"I better hurry up if I want to board the Mexico City Company. What time is it?" asked Antonio.

"You have time my friend; you still have two hours before the whistle blows."

"I want to be at the post early enough to choose a coach with upper class traveling passengers. You know they are the only people able to carry a civilized, deep conversation that is interesting enough during trip," Antonio bragged.

"Has Father Patricio come looking for me lately? Don Julio asked, "Go and tell him I am here!"

Mariano nodded his head and ran downtown to the church. After breakfast, Antonio got his luggage and bid farewell to Don Julio. He turned to the corral trying to take a good look at Leonardo for the last time.

"Amigo, keep your part of the deal, and you will be rich for life. I will bring your share as soon as I close the transaction." Antonio said, "I've had enough of this deserted, arid land. Oh! I miss the city so much!"

"When do you think I will see you again?" Don Julio asked.

"As soon as I find a buyer for La Casa Grande, I will come to Guanajuato."

"I trust you Antonio. We have a lot at stake! Don't let me down," Don Julio warned.

"You have nothing to worry about. I am a man of honor. Now remember! As soon as you are able to distinguish who will prevail, join them. You know what I mean. I will let you know what I see or hear from my end," Antonio replied.

"Realists are in control. We need to sit down and see how strong the secret insurgent movement is. The last thing I heard was about a meeting in Queretaro. Word got out that an uprising would break out by the end of the year. I am sure the Spanish army will crush them, but just in case, I have connections on both sides. We need to join the party that will let us keep the most," the Hacendado explained.

"Be cautious and mute about it. Joaquin trusted his secret to the wrong person, and you know what happened," Antonio warned.

"We need to befriend insurgent leaders like Corregidor Dominguez and General Allende, but at the same time, Realist watchdogs like Corregidor Reaño and General Callejas."

"Go and have peace of mind. You are a good businessman," Don Julio added cynically. His treacherous lips were a tomb for his lying desires. Zenón took Antonio to the post station. By the time the smith came back, Don Julio had already seen all the expenses in the record book. Zenón could tell there was trouble when he looked at the bosses' semblance.

"You have spent three pesos above the budget! I need a detailed explanation, and it better be a valid one!" Don Julio said with a threatening tone. His eyes were full of emotion and fixed on the skinny figure that reluctantly approached the Hacendado.

"Let me show you, I...I ... I bought enough nails and rope for the shop. I also needed a hammer," replied Zenón in a nervous tone.

"Show me proof of it! I know how much that costs and three pesos seems too much for only those three things!"

"Let's see...I had another expense, but I will pay you with my work!" exclaimed Zenón begging for a deal. Don Julio grabbed him by the neck and pushed him against the wall. It was his way of keeping control of what he thought he owned.

"I call the shots here! You need my permission before spending my money! You will pay me back right now! Do you understand? I trust you with my shop and my currency, and you take advantage of it! You are a fool if you are trying to rob me!"

"Sorry sir, I... I had to pay the doctor. María Del Socorro was sick! She was dying, and I was desperate! You have a daughter too! You know how it feels to see her suffer! Please have mercy on us! I will pay you!"

"Leave my father alone!" A young voice called from outside.

It was Mariano who rushed in and stared directly in Don Julio's eyes. Don Julio lifted his hand and hit him on the right cheek, dropping him in his tracks. Leonardo who had heard the argument from the kitchen ran into the room just as the man was lifting Mariano to his feet.

"Please Don Julio, don't hurt them. I will pay you the money!" exclaimed Leonardo.

"You will pay me? Do you have three pesos on you?"

"No, but I do have them back at La Casa Grande."

"You don't have a cent, or…Ah, but maybe you do. You have a beautiful horse! How about if you pay me with it? But why do you want to intercede for these indios? They are thieves and I will never trust them!" wailed Don Julio. "That will teach you to never raise your voice to the one who feeds you! Next time, I will hang you from a tree," warned the big man turning to Mariano. "Did you find the priest?"

"He said he would be here as soon as he could," responded Mariano with resentment.

Don Julio knew that Mariano could bring him trouble if he allowed him to get away with his defiant attitude. He had already told his bodyguards to be on the alert in case there was a surprise.

When the priest arrived, he gave Don Julio a list of people he had seen during confession; in exchange, Don Julio gave him a small purse containing three pesos. It was an agreement they had. Don Julio would learn from the priest who had taken money or provisions and had confessed the sin. Don Julio would demand payback with work time, perpetuating service to their children after a beating, if peasants couldn't honor the debt. The owner of the grant, the Hacendado, collected tribute from the peasants and miners in gold, in kind, or in labor.

At the stable in the back of the shop, Leonardo began to sympathize with Mariano.

"That wasn't right! Why does he treat your family like that? Does he own this place?"

"He is powerful, he owns the whole pueblo!" replied Mariano, "but sooner or later someone will make him pay and make him miserable to his grave."

"But he doesn't own your lives. You should find employment somewhere else. You deserve respect! Your father should notify the Corregidor about his abuses." Mariano changed the conversation. He knew it was risky to talk about Don Julio. At least at this time, he did not want to reveal his own plans. It was his mother's pleas and prayers that held him back from using the musket he had stolen from the Hacienda.

"I see how much you care for this horse. Maybe one day, I will have enough means and pay you back," Mariano said gratefully.

"Oh don't worry about it. I did not agree to his side of the deal. I told him I would pay him but not with Lightning. This horse is my family. My father gave him to me. He is a loyal friend, but I plan to keep my word. I will pay him as soon as I return to La Casa Grande, my real home," Leonardo answered.

"Where are you from? Is Don Julio related to you?" asked Mariano.

"No, but he knew my father. My father paid him to take care of my education before he passed away," Leonardo said with a knot on his throat.

"I am sorry about your father," Mariano added troubled by Leonardo's agreement to pay the family debt. He felt hesitant to trust Leonardo since he was somehow associated with Don Julio. Nevertheless, there was a natural friendship between the two.

"And who is this young man?" asked the priest who was coming out of the house followed by Don Julio. "He looks like a Vallejo, is he Joaquin's son?"

"No, he...he is Leonardo Valle. I hired him to tend my horses, especially that beautiful white colt. It is my daughter's birthday present," Don Julio said, gesturing toward Lightning.

"Did you hire him from La Casa Grande?" inquired the priest trying to confirm his mistrust.

"Yes, he comes from La Casa Grande. As a matter of fact, he knew Joaquin very well. But as any young man, he has to forge his own future and look out for himself. He is good with horses, and since I needed someone to tend mine, I hired him. Like any other peasant, he is under my disposition. I am responsible for him."

"Just make sure he becomes a faithful believer," replied the priest knowing that there was something different about this young man.

"I need to get my baggage ready. I will see that everything is in order for my journey home. It was good seeing you," said Don Julio as he turned to the front of the house.

Just then, he realized Leonardo might say more than he needed, so he turned calling him to come to the front too.

"Don Julio is calling you. I think you are leaving. Come and visit us whenever you have a chance," Mariano said.

Leonardo walked Lightning to the carriage in front of the house. He wanted to make sure the horse had enough rope to follow comfortably. Don Julio had ordered his men to keep an eye on the young man every time he was close to the beast. As Leonardo passed by Father Patricio, he nodded, acknowledging his presence and vocation. The priest instantly knew he had one more soul to save.

"Young man, California is a beautiful land with great ranches and amazing shores. Horses run freely, and the people are friendly. It is a land of opportunity. Moving there can bless not only your life but also your posterity. I lived there for five years in the Misión San Juan Capistrano when the new church was built. I can help you get there," the priest said.

"How do you know me? Did you know that my father wanted me to go to Europe to study and become a doctor? Don Julio has been asked to prepare me for that. There is a teacher in his home, and I am going to take lessons from him."

"I knew Joaquin very well. You can find me here if you need me! I can help you get away! You can trust me on that! Have a good trip muchacho!"

Father Patricio had to be quick and secretive about his conversation with Leonardo. He knew that sooner or later the young man would come to him. Don Julio looked at Leonardo, trying to read his conversation with the priest. It was the first time that he began to worry about the truth. Leonardo's presence in his house was going to bring questions from visitors.

"The young man might say too much about his origin. The stables might be the best place for him to lodge. But what about the teacher?" he thought, "I told him he was going to be taught by a professor! Carmelo de la Cruz is teaching Beatriz right now. It is inconceivable to have a Mexican join my daughter in the house."

As he studied it in his mind, he came up with a plan.

"That's it! I will have Arnulfo, my veterinarian, teach and prepare Leonardo at the stables. After all, the young man wants to be a doctor."

Leonardo was feeling uncomfortable by the way the man looked at him.

"My friend let me give you some advice. Once in my Hacienda, you can say that you come from La Casa Grande. However, it would be better for you to say that you are not Joaquin's son because he had too many enemies. I don't want anybody to try to take revenge and hurt you or anyone in my family. For your own safety, it is better to keep it between us. Do you understand what I mean?" Don Julio asked.

"What enemies? My father was a righteous man. He never took advantage of anyone. I do not understand it. If he owes, I want to see the legal notes, and I will pay."

"Listen, maybe you are too young to understand. Right now, there are wolves around trying to devour anybody's gold. Since the safety of my family is at stake, you will avoid talking about the matter. Is that understood?" the Hacendado demanded.

"I will not cause you any trouble, but I will never hide who I am and where I come from. My father would be offended if he were present."

"We have to be careful! I am not going to risk it. From now on you work for me. I will say that I hired you to care for my horses. You will learn from Arnulfo, my personal horse doctor. You will stay in his quarters at the stable and follow his orders," Don Julio explained.

Leonardo didn't complain or ask any questions because to him that meant being close to the white stallion; nevertheless, he had no idea of what was coming. He thought the journey was bound to be more tolerable now that Antonio wasn't around to threaten or discriminate. Ahead lay the same brown grass, patched fields, and dry September soft winds.

The Hacienda

After many hours of monotonous, arid scenery, there was finally a distant sign of civilization. Far at the end of a slanted field, the dirt road seemed to come to rest into a plantation's grove. It was the Cieneguilla Hacienda. It was the Hacendado's headquarters for the region. It was the place where Don Julio's orders were executed. The vineyards and the peach tree aroma sweetened the dusty wind, but the barbed wire fences admitted the subtle imprisonment. Leonardo looked through the back window, figuring out the way he had come in, just in case he needed to flee right out. The noise of barking dogs and startled turkeys was a sign to Don Julio that he was home.

"Home, sweet home," sighed the Hacendado, "So let's review our agreement. You work for me, and that's what I want you to say! It will be the best way to protect you and my family. You will get along fine with Arnulfo. He is the best doctor in the region. As soon as he teaches you all he knows, you will be ready to enroll in any university in Europe. I want to hear that you obey his commands precisely. You will have a busy schedule, enough to keep you out of trouble. I don't allow far away trips or visits without first consenting to it."

"Where can I go? You are the only acquaintance I have. Don't worry! I will do my best and pay attention to your counsel. My Dad's dream was for me to become a doctor, and I will give my greatest effort to achieve it. Thank you for bringing me to your home," Leonardo replied.

"Look! That's my lagoon. It is deep enough and holds water all year round. There! Behind that grove is home. The stables are on the other side of the corral. By the way, it is my daughter's birthday. It's been her dream to have a white horse. I just haven't been able to find the right one. She is not an experienced rider, that's why I have to select the right horse for her. I've been talking to some friends in Andalucía, but they have not gotten back to me. I believe this one is perfect for her to learn to ride. I see how much you know about horses; do you mind if she uses your horse for a while?" Don Julio asked.

"No one besides me has ever been on Lightning. He doesn't know anybody else. It's risky. She might get hurt. Why can't she use another horse?" the young man proposed.

"As I already told you, she dreams of having a white colt. It is not here yet. I'm asking it as a favor. It is her birthday. Don't you want to please her, too?"

"My horse is the only thing my father left me. He's like a friend to me," Leonardo explained feeling uneasy about the proposal.

"I am not going to take it away from you. The people at the stable will care much better for your stallion if they see my daughter ride it," the man said.

"Mmm, I am not too excited about it. She would need to be around him and even pet him for some time. I think it will work if I go along," said Leonardo.

"Then you will do it together until the day before the big celebration. The Jaripeo is coming up in ten days. I want my daughter to feel comfortable riding by herself. Don't get me wrong, she is very smart and knows a thousand things. But it is those thousand things that have gotten in the way and have not allowed time to ride. Thank you my friend," Don Julio explained.

The carriage finally came to a stop. Everyone felt relieved to be on their feet again. As Don Julio entered the corridor, a tall woman approached him from the side.

"I am so relieved you are home! We missed you so much!" the woman said.

"Where is Beatriz?" asked Don Julio as he hugged her, "I have a surprise for her. She turns seventeen tomorrow, and she would not forgive me if I forgot."

"She is inside finishing her lesson. She is such a fast learner. I am going to miss her when she returns to Spain next year," replied Rosa.

"My dear, it all depends on what happens in two weeks," said Don Julio.

"Who is that young man riding with you?" asked the woman.

"Ah, his name is Leonardo. I brought him to help Arnulfo. He will also help Beatriz get ready for the Jaripeo," answered the man.

"You're always on top of things. I will have Lola fix you dinner. The water is ready if you want to take a bath right away," Rosa said.

Leonardo was directly taken to the stables and shown his quarters. He was amazed to see so many horses. His colt was nervous as he walked the little dirt road adjacent to the corral. They stopped at a small adobe house at the end of the stable. It had a gray wooden door with a metal handle. The guide knocked on the door, creating a loud echo that startled the horses in the stalls. A man with a skinny face answered the knock at the door. He looked through a small opening on the door and stared at the visitors.

"What do you want Fermín?" asked the man from inside the house.

"Don Julio wants this muchacho to work with you in the stables. Give him a place to sleep, and make sure he earns what he eats. Let me know if he gives you any trouble."

"Tell the boss not to worry. I will handle him," answered Arnulfo.

The horse whisperer had been born and raised in the Hacienda. Don Julio trusted him because Arnulfo was responsible and had spent all his life working there. He never had any formal medical training but had a special gift for horses. He knew everything about horse managing, tending, and breeding. Some people claimed that he understood their language. Arnulfo's two sons were also great horsemen. They were not only responsible for cleaning and polishing the tack, including harnesses, reins, saddles, and stirrups; but for riding and training the horses for a variety of recreational and sporting equestrian pursuits. Sometimes, even Arnufo's older daughter Elena would come to help feed the young colts.

"You will follow his orders and obey what the boss commanded," demanded the guide turning to Leonardo.

"I am in charge here! I make sure Don Julio's will is done, so don't give me the least excuse to come down on you. Ah, and one more thing! Don't forget to keep me informed about the brown mare; you know what it means to the boss!" Fermín said in an arrogant tone turning towards Arnulfo.

Leonardo stared at Fermín as he passed him. Even though he did not intimidate him, the new comer did not have the smallest desire to go against his will.

"A white, Arabian, Andalusian stallion! Look at that beast!" exclaimed Arnulfo, "in all my years here, we've never had a white one! Is this?"

"Yes, it is my horse. He needs food and a good place to spend the night, or better yet, a new home. By the way, I haven't introduced myself properly; I am Leonardo Vallejo, your newest student. Don Julio told me that you are the best horse doctor in the area. It will be an honor to learn from you before entering medicine school in Madrid."

"A new cowboy is always welcomed here at the stables! I'll see what I can do. For now, take your horse over there in that empty stall. There is plenty of hay. I will go ahead and prepare a place for you to spend the night. We have a demanding day tomorrow," added the vet as he opened the door and walked away.

Leonardo placed Lightning in a stall between two other horses. When he returned to the front of the house he was hesitant to enter. Everything was so new. He felt a little uncomfortable because he didn't know anybody there. Nevertheless, he went in looking for the vet. The house was very spacious and rustic looking. It had been built from stone, wood, and red clay tiles. Once inside, Leonardo was able to see the kitchen in the front. Five rooms surrounded a beautiful patio that comprised a water fountain with a strange looking figure in the middle. Leonardo stared at it, trying to tell its shape. He waited there reflecting on his whole new experience. He missed La Casa Grande, although his father was the boss, the people who worked for him were his friends; especially Esteban. He wondered if he was still in charge and keeping things in order back home. A mix of emotions overwhelmed him, particularly Antonio's claims concerning his father's affairs.

"But how could my father trust such a man? And what about Don Julio who seems abusive and controlling? It doesn't make any sense! I will demand a copy of my father's will! I need to see his signature on it!" As he was there thinking on the matter, a figure approached from one of the rooms.

"Who are you? What are you doing here?" a young man asked.

"My name is Leonardo, I am…I am waiting for Arnulfo to come and tell me where I will be spending the night." At that moment, Arnulfo came and interrupted,

"He will be helping with all the work, he will stay with us. Don Julio ordered it."

"Great! He can start right now. The brown mare is giving birth at this moment, and I came to get you father!" said the tall young man.

"So soon? Hurry Miguel, I need my tools and alcohol. Leonardo, come follow me!" ordered Arnulfo.

Leonardo followed him running towards one of the covered stalls outside the stables. It was dark, and he did not know his way around. He was afraid to trip and miss Arnulfo's direction.

"I need light! Leonardo, go back and tell Miguel to bring the light, then get me a pail with clean water!"

Leonardo went back into the house and found Miguel. They exchanged assignments and got everything ready for the doctor. The mare was old and had complications throughout her pregnancy. Arnulfo had to be extra careful and did everything he knew to save the animal. It was Beatriz' riding horse, the only one she trusted. Don Julio expected the whole family to ride in the festival inauguration. He had made Arnulfo responsible to have the horses trained. It would be a tragedy if the mare died because Beatriz had never ridden another horse. Without doubt, Don Julio's fury would be felt by everyone at the stables.

As the hours went by, the only thing to do was to wait. Leonardo couldn't sleep that night. He wanted to learn every single detail. Every time Arnulfo looked at the mare, his hope diminished. She was not breathing normally, and the foal needed to be fed. Miguel had brought milk in a bottle, but as much as he tried, the offspring wasn't responding.

"How does she look, father?" asked Miguel in a worried tone.

"I am afraid it is already too late. Just make sure the foal stays warm and takes the milk" Arnulfo answered.

"When are you going to tell Fermín? He should be awakening soon," Miguel added.

"I will take care of it; just make sure that he doesn't find out for himself!"

Fermín was the top administrator. He was Don Julio's right hand. He was jealous that the boss trusted Arnulfo, but it was Don Julio's passion for horses that kept them close.

The September moon had gone to rest, and the new day's sunrays announced the early tasks in the life of the vaqueros. Leonardo had finally fallen asleep on a pile of hay. Not even the rooster's song disturbed his sleep. Arnulfo anxiously paced back and forth in front of the stable. His mind was fixed on Don Julio's reaction to the news.

"Was the boss aware that the brown mare was too old? Maybe he was and that's why he brought the white stallion? Should I start breaking the horse right away? It will not be ready in a week, but if that's what pleases Señorita Beatriz, I will try. She could use mine if she wasn't so nervous about horses! But what about Leonardo and the new stallion? He mentioned that the horse was his."

Arnulfo couldn't come up with a solution, so he went back to check on the new colt and gave orders to remove the carcass right after Don Julio saw it. He knew he could not wait any longer, so he went straight to the main quarters to share the bad news with the boss. When he approached the front of the Hacienda, a man carrying a rifle on his shoulder met him. It was Fermín who was back from the early round up. He was carrying two ducks and a rabbit for today's lunch.

"What is it Arnulfo? Why so early and why do you have that look on you face?" asked the hunter.

"I am going to see Don Julio; I need to speak to him!"

"Are you out of your mind? He's still sleeping. His journey was long and tiring, and you want to wake him up? I can't let you go inside. Tell me what you want, and I'll tell him at noon when he is up," Fermín said pulling the hair from his thick mustache.

"No, I will wait here until he gets up," demanded the vet.

"I am the Hacienda's administrator, second in command. Only Don Julio commands over me, I need to know everything that happens in the Hacienda. It is my job! You can tell me, that way, I can address it. Maybe you don't even need to bother the boss," boasted the man putting the end of the riffle on the ground.

Arnulfo did not trust Fermín with such a responsibility; he knew how he liked to fire up the boss' head with adulation. He decided to go back to his duties and prepare every detail for the Jaripeo.

"By the way, how is the brown mare doing? Will she be ready for the fiesta next week?"

Arnulfo evaded the question and looked away to the front entrance. He knew that if it were up to Fermín, he would have shot the horse just to make the horse whisperer's life miserable.

"I will swing back later, I am sure he would want to see me this afternoon."

Back at the stables, Leonardo was still sound asleep. The accumulation of the sleepless nights plus all the new experiences, finally caught up to him. On the other hand, Miguel was actively engaged in his duties. He had found a broodmare for the foal and placed Lightning in the corral. Seven saddled horses were ready to be ridden around El Camino Real that led to the rodeo arena. Other riders were also busy training for the big race which closed the coming celebration.

The Jaripeo was a major event. It was held during the seven day harvest celebration. It was also a time to buy and trade goods from the region, especially the sweet honey and the yellow guava that came from Calvillo. Most of the people who attended included the Hacendados's family and their trusted servicemen. The five major estate owners chaired the festivities. This time, Don Julio was hosting it and that meant having more than forty people in his quarters. All the servants and common cowboys stayed in the stables and around the estate that became like a little town. Everyone looked forward to the Jaripeo. Besides politics and fine drinks, it was a time to get acquainted with Guanajuato's new sub-intendant. This was a position directly appointed by the Crown; usually a distant relative to the king was assigned to assist the Corregidor or governor. The mines in Guanajuato had produced the biggest extraction of silver in years and the Crown did not trust any outsiders. The sub-intendant worked under the Corregidor. Since it was a discrete designation by royalty, the sub-intendant preferred to be publicly called Regidor.

At this time, Cirilo del Castillo was the new appointee under the Guanajuato Corregidor. He came directly from Spain and was eager to form new friendships in the colony. Prior to his appointment as sub-intendant of Guanajuato, he lived in Austria for fifteen years serving in the Spanish Army. One of the Regidor's major responsibilities was to collect taxes from all the Hacendados, including Don Julio.

Just like Don Julio, Cirilo shared the same passion for horses. He thought that everyone, including women, should be expert riders. He did not pay much attention to what aristocracy dictated about women and horses. Maybe that was the reason he was sent to the colony. Don Julio had done his research on the family and wished to give his daughter in marriage to Santiago, Cirilo's son. He knew that the Jaripeo was the perfect opportunity to make his move. It just needed to be flawless and accompanied by a good permanent first impression.

First Encounter

When Arnulfo reached the stable, he regained hope when he saw the white stallion in the corral. It was tied to a post, nervously awaiting the new rider. Miguel was waiting for the go ahead word to have his comrade jump on the beast. Arnulfo sat on the fence and signaled to the first cowboy to do his job, but as soon as the rider tried to get close to the stallion, it moved around and attempted to bite the man.

"We need to bring him into the narrow fence just like any other wild horse," shouted Arnulfo.

"But I thought he was already tamed? He seemed very peaceful when I brought him over. Maybe he just doesn't trust el Chato," Miguel shouted laughing.

As soon as el Chato jumped on, the beast became a demon. He jumped and snagged until the rider was on the ground. It was an invitation for the second cowboy to prove his capability. In three seconds, he was on Lightning's back but it took only two to put him on the ground. It was Miguel's turn, and he really was the best horse breaker in the house. Arnulfo was so proud of him and confirmed that he wanted his son to do the job. In that very moment, Don Julio and Beatriz came into the stables. Arnulfo jumped down the fence and turned as pale as a corpse. He wasn't expecting them so early. Just then, he realized that he should have waited outside the Hacienda and should have told the news to the boss.

"There he is! Isn't he out of this world? I told you. I knew you were going to like it. Attention everyone! Señorita Beatriz wants to see her brand new horse! Make sure you give her all your attention! It is her birthday!" announced Don Julio.

"Thank you Papa, you know how much I wanted a white one. It is one of the best birthday presents I have ever received. I will need time to ride. What's his name?" the beautiful, black haired girl asked.

"Oh, you will have to take time every evening until the horse follows you around. You can call it what ever you want," the arrogant man responded, "but let's see how it does. Come on Miguel, start the Jaripeo today!"

The rider wanted to impress the young woman and prove to his boss that the Cieneguilla Hacienda was a strong candidate to win the competition. He brought the horse back to the narrow fence passage and held the reigns tight in his left hand. The other defeated riders held the horse as Miguel jumped on its back. It was indeed a show. The beast kicked and jumped, but the cowboy held on. It ran across the corral, moving its head violently in the air, literally communicating its feelings of rebellion. Miguel held his legs tight to the horse's belly and grabbed onto the reign and hair. Six long seconds elapsed, and the rider held on. Slowly, the horse was yielding. Then it leaned forward in a dash and kicked with its hind legs, throwing the cowboy on his back. The stallion neighed and stood on two legs then ran away towards Don Julio and his daughter.

"Oh, father, I am not ready to ride this horse, not me," the young woman nervously exclaimed. Don Julio was puzzled and mumbled,

"But I don't understand, it was so meek and…"

Right at that very instant someone came shouting. "Lightning! Lightning! Relax, calm down."

It was the real owner who came running into the corral and jumped in front of the beast that trotted victoriously.

"What is going on? Who took him out of the stable?" demanded Leonardo.

"I'll serve you dinner if you last longer than six seconds," challenged Miguel in an arrogant tone. Leonardo looked at Miguel with the intention to scold him for taking his horse; but as he turned, he was stunned by the presence of an attractive girl who was looking at him from the benches. There was a warm feeling in his chest stirring his heartbeat with greater energy. He didn't even notice Don Julio sitting next to her. He was love struck and forgot his anger.

"Who is that lovely señorita?" asked the newcomer in a friendly tone.

"Don't even think about it. She is too much for you! Can't you see Don Julio sitting next to her?"

Miguel explained. "Is that…," Leonardo began to ask.

"Yes, that's Beatriz, Don Julio's daughter," Miguel interrupted Leonardo.

"You better start cooking right now, amigo!" said the newcomer jumping on the horse to smoothly ride around the corral.

The horse was friendly like a lamb and began to dance around a known rhythm. Horse and rider knew each other just like water finds its course down the river. Leonardo behaved like a real conqueror, emerging through the crowds, on his way to honor royalty. Everyone was astonished to see the horse's reaction. Miguel stopped keeping track of time as Leonardo rode around the corral. The rider even ordered the horse to kneel down and it obeyed.

"Bravo! Bravo! Now we are ready for the jaripeo," shouted Don Julio.

"That's Leonardo my new horse trainer, and he will dedicate all his time and efforts to help you get acquainted with the horse. Are you still afraid? Beatriz nodded and tried to identify the rider. She thought he was too arrogant to be a servant in the Hacienda. Leonardo dismounted and walked the horse towards Don Julio but looking straight at Beatriz.

"It will be a pleasure to help you get ready for the Jaripeo," he said.

Don Julio stood up and walked towards the fence to take a closer look at the horse.

"Come with me darling, don't be afraid," he shouted.

Beatriz walked down the bleachers fighting with the morning breeze that played with her black hair. Her eyes were fixed not on the horse but on Leonardo who stood in his best posture. As she got closer, the rider began petting his horse, even warning him to behave if she attempted to touch him.

Everyone observed intently as Beatriz extended her hand towards the horse. Arnulfo seemed to be imploring for heavenly help but hesitated to talk to the boss.

"That's my daughter! You are brave like your father," called Don Julio.

He felt on top of the world when his daughter put her fingers through the horse's hair.

"In a few days, it will be hard to decide which one you will ride, this white stallion or the brown mare.

"My princess this is Leonardo. He will help you get acquainted with the horse. He is responsible for getting you ready for the big festivity. He is at your command," affirmed the Hacendado staring at Leonardo in a jealous manner.

"Leonardo, it will be your responsibility to behave like a real caballero, and see that Beatriz feels comfortable with the beast. You have to understand that sometime during the day; I will be trusting you with my daughter. She will need one hundred percent of your attention. Is that understood?"

Once face to face, Beatriz was tense, but Leonardo felt as if he knew her from a long time ago. The girl did not know what to say. She smiled and acknowledged the agreement with a nod.

"Don Julio! Señor, I need to let you know about the mare," Arnulfo said attempting to get the news out of his chest.

"But a minute ago it was a wild horse, we could not break him in!" interrupted Miguel looking at the calmed, friendly animal, "That's a real loyalty lesson!"

"What about the mare? Did she have the foal yet?" inquired Don Julio.

"Did everything go all right with my horse?" interrupted Beatriz.

All the eyes were upon Arnulfo who sometimes moved his hands like if he was telling his side of the story, and a few seconds later words came out of his mouth.

"Señor, I came to see you this morning…I mean, earlier this morning to tell you that it was a very complicated situation. The foal is fine, already running, and I am sure it will become a great race horse but…"

"What about the mare? Did she survive the birth as old as she was? The boss demanded.

"No, that's what I was going to explain; the mare was too old and she did not make it" replied the horse whisperer gasping for air and rubbing his sweaty hands.

"THAT CAN'T BE TRUE! THAT CAN'T HAPPEN AT THIS TIME! It complicates everything. Arnulfo, you failed me! I needed that horse for the jaripeo, we must give a good impression and I needed that horse!" yelled Don Julio as Arnulfo lowered his head.

Beatriz ran to the stables followed by Miguel and Leonardo. They found the dead horse covered with a blanket. Anyone could sense the deep sorrow in the animal kingdom at the stables. The other horse tenders knew they could not remove the corpse, until Beatriz said good bye. She was sobbing like a child. Although she did not ride often, that horse was dear to her. It was a birthday gift when she turned ten years old. Don Julio rushed right after. He was furious about his luck. After a comforting hug to his daughter, he asked Miguel and Leonardo to take his daughter to see the foal. He wanted to speak to Arnulfo without Beatriz being present.

"You will be hurting all your life if Beatriz doesn't ride in the main event. I will send your daughter to the mines in Guanajuato! My prosperity will not be shattered because of your carelessness! Do you realize that Beatriz is the hope of my family and even for all of you in the Hacienda? You better use all your faculties to prepare the best horse! I pay you for that. Do not disappoint me again!" the Hacendado threatened.

"Yes, sir," responded Arnulfo feeling the world upon his shoulders.

Don Julio walked towards his daughter and Leonardo for final instructions. He wanted them to start riding the horse the following day. He also wanted to make sure that his daughter somehow would realize the urgency to be ready, without revealing his subtle plans.

"This foal will become a great horse, just like his mother" affirmed Don Julio,

"We have plenty of good horses, and it's just a matter of getting to know them and getting them to trust you darling. You will start with a new one tomorrow after breakfast. Make sure you have the colt ready Leonardo!"

"I will be here! I can understand what it means to lose your horse," added the young man turning to Beatriz.

They left for a birthday celebration full of presents and carefully prepared meals. As they walked by the corral, Beatriz took a good look at the white stallion. She didn't think it was good enough to replace the brown mare. Nevertheless, she was content to be out of the house, and to interrupt long boring lessons about lady-like behavior and violin. Her teacher's words contradicted her father's approval for a woman to ride a horse.

"I can't understand why am I worried to train with that arrogant new comer? He is just another servant, what can possibly happen? I have my father's consent," she puzzled.

Back at the stables, Arnulfo had made a list of all the major arrangements and preparations needed for the big event. He assigned every cowboy to a team according to the type of competition. He took Leonardo aside and put a heavy yoke on him with his explanation.

"Look, Leonardo, I need to make sure you understand what is really going on. Do you truly know who Don Julio is and what he can do? He owns people's destiny. He is only accountable to the Regidor. You and I want to please him and have him for a friend. We need to win every event in the Jaripeo because the new peninsular will be here, and the boss needs to prove that he is better than the other four. Better as a person, as an administrator, better in products, better in marketing, better because of you and me. He wants you to help his daughter with your horse. I know it is your horse because I know about horses, but please! I beg you! Let her believe it is hers. I will give you any three other horses of your choice if you want."

"I already agreed to do that, what else can I do to help?"

"Great! My boy, I needed to hear that, but it is not enough. You need to get the job done. That's what really matters. Don't let me down because my family will be separated if we fail," explained Arnulfo.

"Has he threatened to do that if we don't win? You've got to be kidding me! It is only a competition. I don't understand his motives," complained the young cowboy.

"For us it is more than a competition because he will send my daughter to work in the mines if we fail. That's why you must take your assignment seriously. My family is at stake."

"I give you my word; I will not let you down," Leonardo replied.

That evening at Don Julio's mansion, an extravagant reception was held to honor his daughter. Invitations were sent to the other four Hacendados, but only Ramon Fuentes and his family from El Tequesquite Hacienda attended the celebration. Ramon had three sons and three daughters, and he was also looking for a good match for his daughters. Among the other Hacendados, he was closer to Don Julio and sometimes sided with his decisions and comments when there was a disagreement. He was also looking forward to el Jaripeo. Ramon had advised some of his close men to spy on the preparations. Right after dinner, Don Julio called their attention and made an audacious statement.

"Ladies and gentlemen, amigos, and familia! Today, we are gathered to celebrate my daughter's seventeenth birthday. We are grateful for your presence and for one more year of her life with us. All of you are aware that she is my only descendant and as beautiful as she is; just like her mother, she will one day inherit all my assets. She already is a qualified administrator. She knows how to balance income and expenditures in the estate. Whoever is fortunate enough to marry her, will one day enjoy all my possessions as well. Of course, he will have to pass a detailed evaluation by me and would need to be as clever as Beatriz. I have a feeling that after the Jaripeo there will be a strong candidate. Please accompany me in singing to her "Las Mañanitas" and wish her happy birthday.

After that, we will be honored to hear her perform a new piece of music."

Horse Riding

Leonardo spent the night thinking about the morning with Beatriz, rehearsing different conversations to keep her entertained. He even thought about how to save her in case she fell from the horse. At dawn, he concluded that he was going to play it by ear and finally fell asleep, only to be awakened by the rooster's song. He got up in a hurry and finished his chores, desperately waiting for the main assignment. He was aware Don Julio had guests in the Hacienda, and that there had been a celebration late into the night. He had the horse saddled already. The sun on his back only increased his restlessness. He approached Lightning expecting the beast to fully cooperate when the girl rode him.

It was about nine o'clock when Don Julio and Beatriz showed up at the corral. They were accompanied by Ramon, his daughter Estela, and his two sons Francisco and Eleodoro. Fermín followed behind and seemed annoyed that nobody informed him about yesterday's events.

"You are finally here!" Leonardo muttered to himself and tried to make eye contact with Beatriz.

"Good Morning! Let's get started now! Leonardo! Bring the horse closer so my friends can take a good look!

Isn't he a beauty? Beatriz will impress everyone on this stallion," Don Julio boasted.

Everyone loved the horse. Estela immediately asked Beatriz for a horse she could ride to accompany her.

"It is a good looking horse, but is it fast enough to compete in the race or just a riding horse?" asked Eleodoro in a challenging tone.

"You have to understand this is my daughter's horse. It might not be fast, but a dear pet for her," explained Don Julio, "Now, get on it darling!"

At first, Beatriz did not move, and then slowly, she entered the corral. There were three reasons why she hesitated. The young woman was nervous about how the horse was going to respond, she didn't feel comfortable having an audience, and she did not want to disappoint her father. Somehow Leonardo's presence gave her confidence and although she refused to admit it, she was a little attracted to him.

Leonardo helped Beatriz on the beast. The horse was nervous too; therefore, his master had to walk alongside pulling the rope. After a ride in the corral, the audience began to clap.

"Excellent! Bravo! Now, try to let her ride alone," shouted Don Julio.

As Leonardo handed the rope to Beatriz, he noticed that her eyes begged for him to stay so he immediately opposed.

"Let's not rush! The horse is barely getting comfortable. I am going to walk beside them!"

The boss felt uneasy that his order was taken as a suggestion. Without notice, he rushed inside and took command.

"Young man, move away! She will be fine!" he commanded with an angry voice.

When the beast felt the intruder and his master going away, he began to trot away towards the other side of the circle. Beatriz hung on tightly to the saddle. She felt an adrenaline rush move like river rapids inside her veins. Don Julio noticing his mistake motioned Leonardo to calm down the horse.

"Alright, this is what you do for a living, and that's why I pay you. This beast follows you better than me. Do your job, I will not interfere," directed the young woman's father.

"Why don't we leave them for a while so I can show you my other colts and cattle Ramon?"

It was now up to Leonardo and Beatriz to finish. They continued to walk and ride around the circle. The horse was still nervous, but little by little, the cowboy moved away. Beatriz was excited to lead the stallion. She wondered how different the beast would react outside the corral without Leonardo present. After a while, the girl and the horse trusted each other. It was time for a little rest. Leonardo approached the rider in the middle of the corral. For a moment, they did not know what to do or say. Leonardo stopped the horse and motioned for the girl to dismount. As he helped her down his eyes were fixed on hers. Unexpectedly, the horse moved away and Beatriz slipped and fell. Leonardo moved quickly and caught her with both arms. Surprisingly, they ended up in each others arms. A brand new world was born in that instant. Illusions and feelings emerged in their tender hearts. It was the seed of love beginning to sprout with sequoia possibilities. Estela, Beatriz' best friend observed attentively. She observed something different about the couple. Once awakened from that instant magical moment, Beatriz and Leonardo walked towards the door.

"Be ready to continue early tomorrow," Beatriz confirmed. "Come Estela, let me show you the elegant outfit samples on the newest publications."

After they walked out, Estela was curious and couldn't wait to ask,

"What's going on between you too?" "Does your father know?"

"What do you mean? There is nothing going on with anybody," Beatriz responded defensively.

"The little Mexican vaquero and you, I noticed how you looked at him,"

"How? Are you joking? I don't see anything in him. He is like any other person. As a matter of fact, he is neither my type nor my class. I will never do a foolish thing like that! Besides, my father would kill me if I set my eyes on a servant," Beatriz said with fake dignity.

"You have to admit that he is more than a servant, he looks refined and well trained. He is also very handsome!" added Estela with a giggle.

Leonardo stood by the fence staring at the girls who walked away. He was still speechless, or otherwise, stunned by what had happened. It was very clear what course of action was to follow.

"It was an awesome move! You calculated every step and moved away exactly at the right moment! Now I am in debt with you!" the rider said to the horse just like a friend says to another.

Ramon and his family left that afternoon shortly after lunch, but they promised to be the first ones back for the Jaripeo. His spies felt comfortable about the rodeo competition. Ramon also left with the clear impression that Don Julio was not interested in arranging matrimony between his daughter and one of his sons. His thoughts were troubled since he heard the host's speech the night before. Fermín accompanied them for about four hours. Once in El Camino Real, he left to Teocaltiche on a visit to Zenón and Mariano. He had been commissioned to collect three pesos from them.

The next morning Beatriz showed up at the corral accompanied by Martina her servant and confidant, only three years older than her. Beatriz was dressed in a dark riding habit with long sleeves. Her clean gloves contrasted her dusty low-heeled brown boots. This time, she was more confident than her first encounter with the horse. She even asked Martina to go home. Fermín followed a few steps behind. He had been ordered to assist and supervise the boss' mandates. Despite the fact that he had a busy trip and little sleep, he was zealous to comply with every order. Leonardo, who had been trotting around, immediately stopped and came to the entrance.

"I am glad to see you again!" He had the whole night to find and rehearse his best greeting. When he was ready to help Beatriz mount the beast, a loud rusty voice startled him.

"Hold your horses cowboy! Don't assume or volunteer unless I tell you," demanded Fermín with fire in his eyes. "Move away!"

He then changed his countenance when he turned to Beatriz. Extending his hand, he offered to help as he held the reins, "Señorita."

As soon as Fermín rushed to help the stallion became wild again. It violently pulled away and stood on two legs, threatening to attack if molested. There was something about that man the colt disliked.

"Ooh! I hate that animal!" Fermín balked with disappointment.

Leonardo took hold of the rope and calmed the horse down.

"What's the matter? Did he forget me already?" the girl inquired looking intensely at Leonardo.

"He needs to go away," demanded the young man pointing to Fermín.

The administrator's pride was broken down. No one in the entire Hacienda had dared to ask him to leave except the boss. The young man's comment was the drop that spilled the water.

"I am going to show you who I am AND YOU ARE GOING TO RESPECT ME FOREVER!" roared Fermín running to grab Leonardo's shirt.

"Stop! Please! You need to leave the corral!" Beatriz begged trying to stop the man. My father trusts Leonardo and I trust him too."

"Just because you are here and you asked me to leave him alone, I will give it a rest for now. I'll make it up to you sooner or later cowboy," Fermín threatened.

Leonardo shook his head. He clearly comprehended the threat Fermín represented.

"Not even Don Julio reacts in such a way. I have to find a way to calm things down!" He thought.

The stallion was peaceful now that Fermín sat on the benches outside the corral. Beatriz mounted with Leonardo's help and rode around by herself. After a few rounds, it was time to trot around.

"I think you are ready to ride outside the circle. Afterwards, I want to show you some tricks," Leonardo said admiring such a pleasant scene. Beatriz pondered why she desired to run through the open fields. It was like a need of freedom from the Hacienda and all its expectations. She gazed outside the gate towards the stables. She knew the open field was just beyond the creek that led to the lagoon.

"It won't take me that long to reach the lagoon, furthermore, I need to prove my riding skills in the open field," she reasoned.

It was perfect timing because Fermín had fallen asleep on the benches, and she was certain Leonardo would play along. In a matter of seconds, she charged like a bullet running through the stables and out the Hacienda. Her gleaming black hair waved good bye to an incredulous Leonardo.

"Wait! Where are you going? Wait for me!" Leonardo ran for another horse, but by the time he rushed out the stables, she was gone.

"That was fast! Either I'm a great teacher, or the horse just likes her now! I like her now, I am going to find her," concluded the young man. The fresh morning wind caressed the early autumn leaves, adding a touch of romance as he sought to find her by the creek.

"Where did she go? I need to find her soon!"

He got off the horse and studied the hoof tracks on the ground. They pointed south adjacent to the creek, a new territory for the cowboy. He had to follow slowly.

"What if she fell? What if Lightning went wild again? What if Don Julio finds out? I better use my last resource," he thought.

His last resource was whistling for the stallion. It never failed. Shortly, he heard a neigh and a gallop. It was a sign the beast was coming to his master, but without a rider.

"Oh no! Where is she? Take me to her!"

He tied the other horse to a nearby bush and mounted Lightning. Now, it was a quest to conquer the dragon and to rescue the princess. A minute later at full gallop, he gazed up to see a thrilling view. She was standing near the lagoon shore. He stopped the horse and jumped to the ground. Beatriz acknowledged his presence and motioned to stay still.

"I love swans. Aren't they gorgeous? Do you know what I like most about them?" the girl asked gasping for air.

"What? Their white feathers? Maybe their long curved neck?" added Leonardo with a puzzled look.

"Their freedom to swim, to walk, or fly anywhere. Sometimes I wish I was one,' she explained.

"You say it as if your life is a prison lacking purpose, or if you were worth less than a bird," Leonardo replied.

"Birds have the freedom to choose whatever they want to eat, whenever they want to fly away, where they will nest, and more importantly who their partner will be. I don't!"

"Have you chosen one and your parents don't approve of him?" inquired Leonardo with the intent to find out where he stood in her life. "No, but I know I am my parents hope for economic stability, and they will arrange my marriage with their best gamble. It doesn't matter what I feel or say. Such is my lot and the lot of women in this world."

"I would never do that to my daughter" replied the young man.

"Promise me that you will never marry anybody for financial convenience, promise me now!" she demanded in a begging and then demanding tone.

"I give you my word," answered Leonardo, "but we need to get back to the house. Give me your hand I will help you up on the horse."

With another hop he was also on horseback. She felt uncomfortable but protected when he put his arms around her waist. Even though she was embraced, just for an instant she felt free. Both knew they were risking it. Don Julio would never approve such a romance.

Back at the corral, Fermín was furious because he had fallen asleep at his post and had no idea where Beatriz was.

"Oh heavens! Someone is here!" exclaimed the girl noticing a black colt tied to a bush.

"Don't worry, that's my horse. I left it here when I came looking for you," replied Leonardo as he jumped to the floor.

"Don't run away, this time wait for me."

The sun was directly above their heads while they continued their way back to the stables. Leonardo seemed troubled. He resolved that his services were not needed anymore since Beatriz had become a confident rider in one day. He was dying to ask if she was going to come back the next day. A negative answer would shatter his dreams. Luckily, no one was at the stables when they left or when they came back. After returning the black colt to its stall, Leonardo gained the courage to ask her.

"I am not willing to spend the whole evening and night wondering about the next day. Will I see you tomorrow?" he asked.

"You still haven't shown me the trick you mentioned. So far, everyone thinks I am an inexperienced rider. Keep that a secret for me," answered the girl.

"I'll walk you to your house," offered Leonardo.

"Just half way, Fermín should be around. I don't want him alone with you."

Beatriz dismounted just past the corral before waving good bye. It was a signal to Leonardo to go back to his place. He stood there for a moment watching her until she entered the portico into the Hacienda. He was already dreaming of seeing her the next morning.

As he walked to the stables just past the corral, an arm grabbed his neck unexpectedly.

"You deserve a beating! I am going to teach you who the real boss is here!"

It was Fermín. He had been looking for him, and this time he was well rested. Both men wrestled to the ground struggling to accomplish their purpose, Leonardo to get loose and Fermín to give him a beating. The irate man was bigger and stronger, but the kid gave a fight. A punch knocked Leonardo to the floor. With anger on his face, Fermín took a whip from the fence and raised it to slash the young man. From the side and without warning, a force struck Fermín throwing him several feet from the young cowboy. It was Lightning in full speed. It was like a bull's force crashing a helpless pumpkin. The beast threatened to charge again. As soon as the man sat up on the floor, he took his gun out. Just an instant before he fired, a voice caught his attention.

"Put the gun down! If you kill that animal you will regret it forever! Don Julio is counting on this horse for the jaripeo! Put the gun down! Don't ruin your life!" It was Arnulfo arriving at a perfect time after he heard the scuffle. Fermín got up and scolded Leonardo without saying a word. He then turned to Arnulfo and said,

"After the big event, I will shoot this animal, and I will send this scoundrel to the mines! You'll see!" He picked up his hat and left in a hurry.

Arnulfo helped Leonardo up and took him inside his house. He asked Elena to bring alcohol and a cloth to clean Leonardo's face. Elena was an attractive, hardworking girl who had certain interest in their guest. Her sweet smile and smooth character invited anyone to become her friend.

"You have to stay away from that man! Make sure there is someone around all the time," warned the vet standing next to the girl, "he will attempt to send you to the mines and we can't let that happen!"

"What are the mines? What happens there?" inquired Leonardo.

"It is the worst place on earth! You won't get out alive! And just in case you get out, you will shortly die of exhaustion and lung infection. Sending someone to the mines is a discrete way to eliminate him. Usually, indentured servants and those who oppose the church are sent there. Believe me, they work until they pay the last centavo and then die!" Arnulfo explained with a shaky voice.

"Do you mean that all the silver my father transported to Mexico City was obtained at the expense of someone's life?"

"Exactly! That's why there are so many contentions around the land. Boys are taken from their families by deceit or by force and become slaves for the Spaniards. They usually have an army to put down any rebellion. Sooner or later the Mestizos and Creoles will seize power and then it will be chaos."

"Will Fermín send me there?" asked Leonardo.

"Only Don Julio can sign the order but Fermín can push him to do it," replied the vet.

"Which side are you on?" asked Leonardo.

"What do you mean?" continued Arnulfo.

"Yes, which side are you on, the Indians or the Spaniards?"

"I wish everyone had the same rights and opportunities. Look, the Hacendados own the land. They have no idea of how much they own. We are beggars at their feet, barely surviving on what falls from their tables. Of course I am an Indian and I suffer all the injustices. But I keep myself away and silent from those things because I love my family."

The next morning Beatriz was on time, and Leonardo showed her how to tap the stallion's shoulder to make it kneel down. Fermín sat on the bleachers with two of his men. There was no way he would allow the riders to leave the corral by themselves, but Beatriz had a plan of her own.

"We need to go back to the lagoon, and this time you have to guide the horse there!" commanded the girl.

"What about your guards?" asked Leonardo.

"Don't worry about them, I already spoke to my father. Let's go!"

As soon as they exited the circle, Fermín got up and approached them. With a haughty look he said,

"With all due respect Señorita; you can't leave the premises if I don't know where you are going!"

"Do you think you are my father? How dare you try to impose your will upon my wishes? You need to go and ask my father if you should be here! Or better yet, I command you to leave my presence and come back in three hours!"

"I have been ordered by Don Julio to make sure you are ready for the jaripeo! That's what I am trying to do," replied Fermín in a defensive tone.

"I will be better prepared if you are not around. Martina and Leonardo will make sure I am fine. See you in three hours!" insisted the girl.

Leonardo held the rope on his way to the stables, and Martina followed along. The men walked away from the scene.

"Martina, wait here with Elena! We should be back soon!" the rider ordered when they passed by Arnulfo's house.

"Yes Señorita, just be careful," answered the maid.

Leonardo secured himself a horse, but again, when he was ready to go Beatriz was gone. This time he knew exactly where to find her. It was a foggy morning, and the cries of some wild ducks echoed through the branches. He had a feeling that this time alone with Beatriz would become a turning point in his life.

From a distance, he saw her endearing presence next to the water. She turned and smiled when he approached.

"I defeated you again! You are too slow,"

"I didn't know it was a race. I expect a rematch tomorrow," remarked Leonardo. "Tell me, what are you planning to do at the Jaripeo?"

"Ride your stunning colt, wave to the crowd, smile, and please my parents!" she answered.

"What should I do? Is there something I need to rehearse?" asked the young man.

"Just stand back and enjoy the event. Every year we ride as a family in the inaugural parade. This year my father wants to extend the parade all the way to the rodeo before his welcoming remarks. Everyone is looking forward to the celebration. You should wear your best attire, and cheer for our cowboys," explained Beatriz.

"Do we have a chance to win it?" asked the young man.

"It's hard to say. Miguel has been first in horse breaking for the past two years, and we are strong in other categories. But the event that really counts is the race. We've never won it. Eliodoro from El Tequesquite got second place two years ago but the people from Guanajuato always take that one. They take every occasion to bring it up. They're so proud," said Beatriz with dislike.

"You speak of them as if they were enemies," commented the young cowboy.

"You will understand when you see them, but it is worse when you get to know them personally. They only think about money and class. For them, Europe is heaven and any foreign born is seen as a fallen angel. I look forward to the day when this land establishes its own government with equal rights for all human beings."

"You wouldn't say that at your dinner table. Where did you learn such a revolutionary idea?" Leonardo questioned.

"I've taken lessons from the best teacher in the world; Carmelo de la Cruz has lived in England and France. He has basically been a tenant in their libraries. He and I envision a republic just like the one of the ancient Greek. But with the rights specified by John Locke where citizens have the right to life, health, liberty, and possessions."

"My parents had the same dream or thought. My father told me of a secret group moving to establish such a country soon. Once, he mentioned General Ignacio Allende and some other people who will bring it to pass. He instructed me to join their cause when the time was right," added Leonardo, "how do you see it happening?"

"There is no way this new country can be established here where there is already an existing powerful ruling system. Officials and hacendados only care about increasing their fortunes through other people's labor."

"But it has been done already, the thirteen United States paved the way," Leonardo explained.

"Yes but not everyone is treated equally! Women and blacks are seen inferior; and the Natives are nonexistent in their government! Unless there is a total change, not only politically but also within the people; I mean a change in the heart and mind of the families, then equality can exist. I'm suggesting an inner change in both rulers and citizens," lectured Beatriz.

"That's one of the main reasons the struggle for independence didn't start here fifty years ago. Sometimes a nation is not mature enough to deserve it," Leonardo explained, "Spaniards don't want to understand Creoles, Creoles don't want to mingle with Mestizos, and Mestizos look down at the Native Americans. Rich and poor don't listen or understand each other, although, they occupy the same land and right to life."

"I agree. They don't even want to share the very air they breathe. Some are too ignorant to know they are ignorant." Beatriz observed, "But some are blinded by all their knowledge and that makes them ignorant as well."

"If such an effort would start tomorrow, what would you do?" asked Leonardo.

"I confess I am afraid the way I would respond. I want my own freedom to choose. I dream of a time when both husband and wife make decisions together. I see my future when I see my own mother and other women, subjected to their husbands will. They are submissive and afraid to contradict because they fear the man they unconditionally love. Is love such a thing? I would not call it love. Love is absent in such relationship. It is fear! Fear to be lonely, to be without a last name, fear to starve to death because they can't provide for themselves or their children. Fear to be without a man because no one will hire them. Fear to go against tradition of treating women as inferior. Fear of the stigma of being a runaway wife and the husband's beatings when found. Regardless of whom I merry, such is my future. Sometimes I want to go far away but where can I go?" lamented Beatriz.

Leonardo looked intensely at her enchanting countenance. His eyes screamed,

"Here I am. I can totally understand. Let me be part of your dream," but his voice hid cowardly.

He took her hand and without saying a word tried to kiss her tender lips. Beatriz was astonished and confused.

"If you trust me, I can take you to a new land where freedom is a reality. Please believe me, I will care for you and will do anything to see you happy. I know it hasn't been long, but the very second…" blurted Leonardo before being interrupted.

She was surprised at such a bold venture. Breaking away she cried,

"What are you doing? This can't be happening, no! Not to me! My father will kill you if he finds out! How will I tell…?"

"That's fear! You are following your fear rather than your heart!" interrupted Leonardo.

"I have to go!" Beatriz cried running to the horse.

Leonardo remained behind watching the rider disappearing into the bushes. He had found a better reason to stay at the Hacienda now.

"When will I see you again?" he thought.

He needed time to ponder her words and his options to convince Don Julio about their relationship.

The thought about a far away place with opportunities to grow could only be defined in one word:

California; a beautiful land with great ranches and amazing shores. A place where horses ran freely and the people were friendly.

"That's it! We can go there, the priest back at Mariano's; he knew what he was talking about! I need to see Beatriz," resolved the young man.

He got on horseback and began his way back to the house. He was surprised to see Beatriz impatiently waiting under a mesquite tree. Leonardo had forgotten that both needed to return together to the stables. He jumped down the horse and ran to her side.

"Please forgive me for what I did, I just…"

"Leave that alone. Don't say one more word about it," interrupted the Hacendado's daughter as she walked towards the house. He followed holding the two animals' reigns on his hands. Beatriz accelerated her pace when a voice startled her,

"Thank heaven you're here! Did it go well today?"

It was Martina who stood with Elena on the stables' entrance. The rich girl didn't answer and continued walking. Elena walked towards Leonardo and grabbed one of the horses. Her striking smile caught him off guard. He stared at her, and thanked her for taking the horse. Right at that moment, Beatriz looked back and froze on her feet. She became aware of a possible opponent, and how her feelings were growing for Leonardo. She did not have the courage to turn away. Leonardo noticed her and waved goodbye. She waved back without thinking about the whole incident.

Choosing Destiny

Early the next day, Don Julio wanted to check every station and event for the jaripeo. He had assignments for all his men and asked for a full report about their progress. He started with the produce sale which included onions, carrots, tomatoes, corn and beans. He was always satisfied with the squash and green and red pepper quality. Of course the guavas, peaches, and the grapes stood out. His vineyards were well known in the area, but it was his cattle that brought the biggest earnings. While he spent the morning visiting with his mayordomo, his administrator did most of the talking. He had a checklist for every single person living in the Hacienda. Two days before the big fiesta was payday. The workers and the administrator would settle their transactions. Each head of household would pay back the cost of the seed they had borrowed. In addition, half of their produce would need to be collected by the Hacienda because they had leased the land they had tilled. Harvest settlement as they called it, took about two days, but most of the goods were sold during the fiesta. Only a few of Don Julio's men knew how to add and subtract. Since he was going to be awfully busy with guests, he needed additional help.

"I will send Leonardo to help in the market during the jaripeo, but make sure you train him and test his math skills," ordered the big boss, "Fermín, remind me to do that when we check the stables later today."

Back at the stables, Arnulfo and his team were timing the race horses. His cowboys were confident about their performance, especially about breaking the wild horses. Arnulfo was worried about the race and only had a remote hope of winning it. He wouldn't dare tell the boss. Leonardo was outside the corral which slowly was becoming a rodeo arena. Most of the events would be held there, but there weren't enough seats. He had waited since the morning, hoping Beatriz would show up. He stood on the bleachers to get a further view of headquarters; however, nobody was coming his way.

He didn't even bring the horse.

"Come on Beatriz! Please come! I need to see you," he despaired.

"My lady is waiting for you in the Lagoon," Martina announced from the stables entrance, "We came earlier but you weren't here. Go now! Don't make her wait anymore."

Surprised with the news, he ran to the stables to get a horse but the white stallion was missing.

"Did she take my horse?" cried Leonardo in a worried tone.

"Of course, that's the whole reason she is seeing you, isn't it?" responded the maid in a sarcastic tone. Without saying a word, he got on horse back and rushed to his favorite spot. After a few minutes, he found her sitting by the shore. The brightness in her eyes was like the sunrays from heaven. His initial desire to leave the Hacienda was slowly diminishing.

"I wasn't sure if you would come. When did you get here?" he asked.

"Today was your rematch to get here first, and I beat you again," answered Beatriz with a charming smile.

"I'll be honest. I fell asleep at four o'clock in the morning. I had too many things on my mind," replied Leonardo.

"What was on your mind?" asked the young woman.

"Many things but mainly you and what happened yesterday. Please forgive me! I have something to tell you but first answer me. Would you trust me again?"

"I never lost trust in you. I wouldn't be here if I didn't trust you."

He was relieved to hear that. It was now his chance to present his bold proposal.

"I've heard of a far away land, a land of opportunity where people are friendly, a place with great ranches and great shores. I would give my life to take you there."

She listened intensely. Scenes of her entire life passed through her mind. Now, a single decision could change the course of her destiny.

"What land is this?" asked the girl in a soft voice.

"Up north to California, the priest in Teocaltiche offered to help me get there. He has lived in one of the missions and I can buy land there. I just need to get back to my father's estate La Casa Grande," explained the young man.

"Are you suggesting that I run away with you? Why would I do such foolish thing? That's not how I want to make the biggest decision in my life. I would want to be in love, then, I would need to be legally wed. And before I face the whole world fighting to stop me, I would try to persuade my parents to be on my side," explained the young woman.

"Do you want me to try and talk to your parents?" suggested Leonardo.

"Are you saying that I am lost in love with you and that you are the right husband for me?" fumed Beatriz.

"I am only hoping that day will come. Will you let me know if it happens?" replied Leonardo in a playful tone.

"Who is your father?" she asked.

"He was Major Joaquin Vallejo. He passed away last month."

All of a sudden a deep grief covered his expression.

"He was killed in the line of duty on the way to Mexico City," the young man explained.

"I am very sorry! What about your mother?"

"She passed away when I was ten years old. But both of my parents are still here in my heart," he said.

"Why are you serving in my house?"

Leonardo remembered Don Julio's command about hiding his identity; nevertheless, he was more faithful to his ancestors and never denied them.

"It was an agreement I had with your father, but I realize that he tricked me. He told me Arnulfo was a veterinarian and that he would be teaching me before I went to the University in Madrid. He is no animal doctor…"

"I know my father. He is quite sneaky with his words. What will you do? Do you plan to stay here forever?" asked the girl.

"I plan to leave after the big event, unless you need me for anything else? I have heard that too many surprises happen during the jaripeo, even marriage agreements. If that is the case, and your father arranges for you to marry an unknown, rich, old man; do not throw you dreams away. It's better to face the whole world trying to live the way you deserve than to leave the world having lived a miserable life," he declared.

His words brought back her fear and uncertainty. All of a sudden, Leonardo's proposal didn't seem like a bad idea.

She was afraid to consider the thought of falling in love with him.

"I sense that your freedom is slowly dying. Do something about it!" begged the young man.

She looked directly to his eyes and said,

"Leonardo, I can't leave with you! Our worlds are very distant. But I am not saying that I dislike you."

There was a joy in his eyes when he heard those words of hope. He put his hand inside her hair and repressed his longing to hold her.

"But will you come with me to California if you need to get away?" asked Leonardo with a rapid heart beat and short breath.

"At this moment my answer is no, and I don't want to talk about that anymore. Why don't we go back to the stable and show my father how much I have improved," suggested the young woman.

As they entered the stables, Don Julio and his men were making an inventory in that area of the estate. He was annoyed to see them coming from the field alone. From far, Leonardo felt an impulse to confront him about his side of the agreement and to ask about seeing Beatriz, but he thought it would be wiser to wait for a later time. The boss was surprised to see his daughter riding by herself. His joy was so great that he left everything and rushed in her direction.

"Magnificent! Just what I needed to see! Can you do full gallop?" he asked.

Beatriz entered the corral riding at a considerable speed. She knew this demonstration would make Leonardo look good. She even made the stallion dance around. Her father was delighted.

"That's my daughter, a complete conqueror just like her father!" exclaimed Don Julio.

"It is Leonardo who deserves all the credit, he has been very patient and helpful to me," said the girl. Don Julio just nodded his head and helped her down. He took her by his side and commenced walking to the main quarters.

"Fermín! Take over! I will be back after lunch."

He needed to reveal his plan to his daughter because she played the most important role. No matter what her feelings and wishes were, she would have to sacrifice in order to take away the financial burden on the family.

Once they got to the main quarters, Don Julio took her to his library and locked the door behind him. Beatriz already knew what he wanted.

"I see that you are old enough to understand what it takes to secure a good life," explained Don Julio, "Your mother and I have great expectations from you. We would do anything to see you happy. The Cortez Family has prestige not only here in New Spain but in Europe also. My parents gave everything they had to educate their children, and look at me; I am the Hacendado in this area. Do you know what that means? The Vice-Royalty trusts me. It has taken me more than thirty years to gain that trust. It took tremendous sacrifice, patience, and work from my parents to leave the mother country and try their fortune here. They invested half of their fortune and even traveled a great distance to secure this piece of land. My parents toiled here and spent their time clearing the way for me to become what I am. I feel grateful to them, but at the same time, I have inherited a great responsibility. I am the third generation with a legacy of success. My sweet daughter, presently, we find ourselves victims of a weak economy. Things are not going well in the country. Trade is scarce, and I'm not able to sell my products at a good price as before. The unstable government and the conspiracy of power hungry aristocrats have caused the ruin of many families. Of course, we are not there yet, but that's the reason I am telling you all this. We are not doing well! Our financial situation is desperate! My investments have yielded very little profit. My debts are slowly biting my savings and my peace of mind. If we don't receive a fair influx of capital, we would lose the estate and all our assets. I would lose the trust invested in me by the government. Most of all, we would be the ridicule of many friends. You my dear, you are my only hope!"

"What do you mean? I don't understand how I can save the situation, the family name, or prestige," puzzled the girl, "I would do anything to make you and my mother safe and happy."

"That's my girl, a real Cortez. Now, let me tell you what I have in mind, and you must follow my plan exactly. Your age is a wonderful age. You are beautiful; you have so many dreams. Next week, Cirilo Del Castillo and his family will lodge with us for a whole week. Cirilo is a great person to know and to have as a friend. He is the new subintendent for the area. He was commissioned by the Crown to oversee the silver from the Guanajuato mines. He is part of the royal family. He has an army at his command and receives taxes from the five Hacendados. I want to become his partner and work for him. Our families need to start a great friendship. His son Santiago is ready to settle down. He graduated from the University of Vienna and received degrees in music and animal medicine. He is also coming. He loves horses. I think you will get along well with him because you have much in common."

"What do you mean in common? I don't even know him," complained Beatriz.

"Not yet, but your assignment will be to host him and become his best friend in these seven days. Make him trust you. I am telling you, if you like him, and everything goes well, Santiago will become a great match for a husband. He is Cirilo's only son and heir to his fortune, and thus, our chance to resolve our financial troubles. Do you understand our situation and how you play the most important role in our future?"

"What if there is no chemistry between us? What if neither of us likes each other? You are putting a heavy load upon my shoulders? What about my life? I always said I would need to be in love before I married anybody," protested Beatriz.

"The most important thing about getting married is finding a good match. Santiago is more than a good match. Love will come later. You will be the happiest woman in the world at his side. Just wait and see. I am pretty sure he will be astounded when he sees you," affirmed the man trying to convince her.

"I don't want him to love me only for my outward appearance. I feel that you are not only rushing but forcing me," she protested.

"Your mother and I have agreed that this is a good direction for your life. You might be too inexperienced to see it now. I'm asking you to try! Think about your mother and me! We have done so much to raise you! We have provided you with the best education and comfort. We have strived all these years just to give you everything. I think we deserve at least a try from you! A good relationship for a week can blossom into something important. Now, go and contemplate it. We'll talk again in a few days," added Don Julio in a commanding tone.

She got up and left immediately. She knew that going against her parent's wishes was just like swimming against the current. Don Julio remained silent in the room. He only had a few days to convince his daughter about his plan. He was already preparing the next step to pressure the girl. He also had put the burden on his wife. He had made her responsible for convincing his daughter. He even threatened to fire all the household servants if she didn't carry out his wishes.

That afternoon, Beatriz did not come out of her room. She stayed in bed pondering about a woman's fate in the world. She thought about all the married women she knew.

"I wonder if they had a word in their marriage arrangement. It is so unfair, but at the same time, I would be ungrateful to disobey my parents! What am I going to do? What about our financial situation? One more headache! Nonsense! Long ago, I made up my mind to never marry anybody for money or social class. I presume my only option is to wait and see what happens during the Jaripeo."

The Prophecy

The next morning someone came into Leonardo's sleeping quarters and forcefully awoke him.

"Get up now! It's time to pay for what you eat!" demanded an angry voice.

Leonardo was shaken by the violent push. He was terrified to see Fermín right by his side.

"There is a hidden wedge between you and me but I will settle that later!"

He immediately remembered that he had threatened to send him to the mines. He felt a little relieved when he saw Arnulfo standing by the door.

"You will be working for the market supervisor now. You will be doing inventory in the storehouse throughout the Jaripeo. Follow me!" demanded the second chief in command.

The young man looked at the man by the door, looking for a confirmation of what was said. Arnulfo nodded in the affirmative but worried that Fermín would hurt the young man on the way, so he stayed around to protect him.

"But I have a commitment with Beatriz, we are still preparing for the jaripeo!" complained Leonardo.

"Señorita Beatriz to you! Never forget she is above you! You are nobody! Isn't it obvious? She doesn't need you anymore!" Fermín affirmed, "I will train her from now on. Hurry up and get going!"

In a brief moment, the three men left the house towards the west side of the estate. Once there, Leonardo was intrigued by the men carrying heavy loads in and out of the adobe storage rooms. These rooms were full to capacity at this time of the year. Most of the grain was put in sacks and piled up to the ceiling. The other rooms contained the fresh produce that needed to be sold or loaned at the moment.

"This fellow will stay here and help you with book keeping. Make sure you check his pockets at the end of the day," commanded Fermín to a man sitting on a table.

He was the supervisor. He was busy writing in a notebook with a thick black ink pen.

"Leonardo! Do you know what the punishment for stealing is?" He asked as he put the pen down.

"You will receive ten lashings and will pay twice as much! Think about that!"

"You will follow his command and don't give any trouble! You are to remain here until he dismisses you at night. Is that clear?" threatened Fermín staring at Leonardo.

"He won't give you any problems, you can trust him," added the horse whisperer standing next to the young man. "I need him back at the stables as soon as possible.... whenever all this is gone."

The four men stared at each other for a moment and then agreed to go back to their chores. All Leonardo thought about was having a little chance to see Beatriz in this place.

"Have you ever used a roman scale?" called the supervisor.

"No sir," responded the young cowboy.

"Come follow me. Pay close attention because you need to weigh all the grain and bean sacks in the other room!"

It was very simple to understand, but not many laborers knew how to write and record the weight. In the first storehouse, there were mountains of pinto bean sacks piled and already counted. Leonardo's job was to weigh and record all the ones coming off the wagons. There were four men weighing and recording while other people unloaded the arriving shipment. The supervisor gave instructions to an older man to train the novice in his assignment.

"Let him see you do a few and then let him try for a while. Make sure you monitor him. He should go to that scale by the door when he is ready. We should receive a new person tomorrow to help you accomplish this task before Saturday."

At the main quarters Beatriz stayed in her chamber until late morning. Martina brought breakfast upstairs.

"I need you to go to the stables and tell Leonardo to be ready at noon," Beatriz commanded.

Martina left immediately but was unable to find the cowboy. No one knew where he was.

The morning went by but it felt like eternity to Leonardo. He was hungry and tired but already working alone at his own station.

"I need to see her again," he thought, "What if she tells her father about our conversations and my proposal? That would be risky. What if all this is a plan to keep me away from her? Did Fermín find out? No, I don't think Don Julio or Fermín know."

With the loads coming and coming, the assignment grew instead of diminishing. Leonardo felt weak and dizzy. He hadn't taken a break since the morning but continued to work because no one on his team stopped. He didn't want the administrator to disbelieve Arnulfos' words. Finally, there was a loud whistle blown and the crew quickly headed for the door. He did not know what it meant but one of the workers advised him to eat well and quickly. Outside the storeroom there was a group of people carrying baskets with food. They were the laborer's family members who had brought a meal to their father or brother. Everyone had something to eat except Leonardo. He thought about running to the stables but just then an older man took him by the shoulder and bid him to sit with his group.

"You don't have anybody who brought you tortillas, do you?" asked the man.

"No, I don't have anybody."

"I am sure we will have enough for all of us. Come with me!"

They sat under a huge alamo tree where a clay jar lay near the trunk. Leonardo went straight for it to quench his thirst. He then was introduced to several young and older men. They were curious about his origin and asked all sorts of questions.

"Are you one of them or one of us?" the leader said.

"He wouldn't be working like an animal if he was one of them?" another man replied.

Leonardo recollected Don Julio's warnings about his background, but he openly told them about his father and La Casa Grande. He had no idea who would bring that information to the administrator and other supervisors in the Hacienda.

"Let me tell you who my mother was and her advice. Many times she talked about her ancestor's visions, the Mexica wise men prophecies. We might be living them at this time. The tradition of the Mexica warned that if there was a time when the forests lost all their leaves, the river's clear flow became weak and tinted, or the puma's claws became dull and weak, such a natural distortion would bring terrible plagues to the land. What do you think this allegory really means?" Leonardo asked the attentive men.

"Was your mother a Mexica native?" one of the workers asked.

"Yes, her name was Techiayotl. A beautiful name! It means esperanza or hope."

"There is no way for all the trees to lose all their leaves! I have heard that the jungle down south is endless!" The leader among the workers shouted, "And even if they do, they will grow back again the following spring. The only way to lose all the leaves is to cut down all the trees, but that is impossible."

"But what about the water being colored? I have heard this saying too! But I haven't been able to figure it out," an older man commented.

"If Fermín keeps shooting all the wolves and pumas not only will their claws be weak, but the whole species will disappear!" a man with a sarcastic attitude exclaimed.

"We have to kill those unnecessary evils! Otherwise they will finish all our cows!" the first man replied.

The last comment made the crowd boil into conversations of all sorts. Leonardo wanted to share his thoughts, but he couldn't get their attention back. He stood up and began his way back to the storage room.

"Wait! You can't leave until you tell us what your mother meant!" the leader demanded in a loud voice.

"Why do you want to know?" Leonardo asked.

"What if the answer pertains to you and requires action against your own way of life? Will you be passive?"

"What are you trying to tell us?" the worker asked.

"Let me put it this way. When men exploit their natural resources for power and greed, they will quickly move on to the exploitation of human beings. We have allowed that to happen!" Leonardo explained.

"Be more specific with your aristocratic way of talking! What are you really saying?" the leader demanded.

"Equal chances for progress are forbidden to us. Most estates have become an elusive imprisonment for our ancestors. Should someone be punished for being born in misery? Why can't he move to the city, or even better to Europe?" the cowboy asked.

"He doesn't have the means to pay or to buy food?" the men answered.

"Should he be destined to stay in his poverty or move to another place where he can find better opportunities?" the cowboy asked. "Hacienda boundaries will soon become country boundaries. They only serve the ones who established them."

"We are born poor and there is nothing to do than to work for bread. No one will feed an idle man!" another man commented.

"That's right, hard work must pay. But in La Casa Grande Hacienda workers were allowed to come and go if there was a better payday somewhere else. We encouraged respect and fairness," Leonardo explained.

"Why did you leave your Casa Grande? If you are one of them, then go back to your wealth and position! Don't come here and eat our rationed food when you have tons in store! Don't pretend to show off when you are just one of us!" the leader howled with deep resentment.

"I say these words because parents always sacrifice their all to give the coming generation a better future. I wanted to feel the water among you," Leonardo said.

"You better be sure of that. We not only give our life for our children, we live it with them!"

"What do the tree, the river and the puma represent?" the other men asked, "Is this allegory referring to us?"

"That's right. It is us," Leonardo replied.

"Who is the exploiting man?" three men asked in unison.

"It all depends if we are talking about the home, the hacienda or the country. Then there is the caste system in place, a domino oppression effect."

After a short time, everyone was called back to work until it was dark. Right before sunset, the supervisor came in to check on Leonardo and his recordings.

"I see that you have done well for today. Not a slacker, are you?" he said sarcastically.

"No sir," replied the young man.

"Go get some rest because we will continue early tomorrow. Don't be late!" commanded the boss, "Be careful about making up stories about your parents. If anybody asks, you tell them you come from the stables. Don Julio already commanded me to keep an eye on you!"

Leonardo nodded and headed to the stables. He was surprised to hear how much power and influence Don Julio really had on people.

As he got to the trail cross, he was able to see the main quarters. His thoughts immediately turned to Beatriz. He stopped for a second and then walked towards her house. It was dark already and some dogs were barking. He thought it would be a good idea to climb up a mesquite tree to get a better look. It was also a hasty way to avoid the dogs in case they found him. After a while, it was completely silent. He realized that the only way to see Beatriz was to come into the house; however, he didn't have a good explanation to be there.

"Come on, think! I need to see Don Julio to ask him about our agreement. No! What if he changes his mind and sends me away from here! But I am a Vallejo; I am not being treated right. No one is treated with respect in this Hacienda," he thought.

"Come on! Think of something good. Why would he get upset if I go to the main quarters? He came to the main quarters in my house!"

All of a sudden, a bright idea came to him. He would come and ask about Antonio. Regardless of his ill manners, he had mentioned that he was in charge of all his father's assets.

"How would I know if he really will pay debts when everything is sold?" he questioned.

He jumped down the tree and briskly walked to the main quarters. As he approached the front corridor, two men came from the main house to meet him. They were the night guards who aimed their guns at him.

"PLEASE DON'T SHOOT! I am Leonardo Vallejo, I am from the stables. I am here to see Don Julio."

"Who is your supervisor and how do you know Don Julio?" shouted one of the guards.

"I lodge with Arnulfo the horse tender. Don Julio brought me over from La Casa Grande. I am staying here to prepare to enter the University in Spain," retorted Leonardo in an agitated manner.

The guards looked at each other and agreed to let him in after he was searched. He had no idea where to go once inside the main quarters. There was a great garden right after the corridor. He continued walking towards the main entrance in the other side of the garden but didn't dare to come inside unannounced. He passed the door and walked all the way to the end of the main building. There was an entrance through the side where the service people came in. He peeked from the door and saw two women busily making cheese. He recognized Martina when she turned her face.

"Leonardo, is that you? What are you doing here?" she asked.

"I am looking for Beatriz, can you call her?"

"Does she know you are here? Did Don Julio give you permission to see her?" interrogated the maid with a worried tone. "I also need to see Don Julio but I need to talk to Beatriz first, just go call her," replied Leonardo.

"Don Julio is not here. He left to Guanajuato. He will accompany Señor Cirilo Del Castillo and his household on their visit here. Let me see if Señorita Beatriz is available. Wait outside in the garden."

He felt very lucky about the boss's trip away from the house. He immediately went to a fountain to wash his face. Through the little ripples in the water, the reflection of the moon finally changed the dark night. He stood there, wondering what had happened after his last conversation with Beatriz.

Moments later, the servant came out of the house and invited him to come. She directed him to go inside the kitchen. Beatriz was impatiently waiting for him.

"Come this way!" Beatriz said taking his hand, "I tried to find you the whole day? I thought you had left the Hacienda! I have been so blind....please forgive me!"

"Don't say more, I don't need to forgive anything. I was at the warehouse all day. I have been assigned to work there. But I thought about you every minute. It's great to see you," interrupted Leonardo.

Holding hands, they continued walking into a patio and stopped by a wooden, polished bench.

"You can't be here long. My father went to Guanajuato, but my mother is in her chamber waiting for me," Beatriz whispered, "I have an answer for you."

Just then, someone interrupted.

"Señorita! Señorita Beatriz! Your mother is calling you," announced Martina.

"What's your answer? Tell me before you go!" demanded the young man.

"Both of you have to go back! Fermín is in the kitchen!" advised the maid.

"I am coming. Just a second!" answered Beatriz.

She got up and looked directly at him.

"I have decided to talk to my father about how I feel about you."

"Don't you think I should know first?"

Without a thought she kissed him and rushed from his side into the house. He was stunned and stayed there trying to hold that instant forever.

"I'll take that as a yes?" he uttered, "When will I see you again?"

She was gone without saying a word. He had to find a way out of the house to avoid Fermín and the guards. The maid bid him to come inside the main corridor and sent him out through the main entrance. As he walked through the house, he was able to see the stairs that led to Beatriz' chamber. He continued down the hall until he got to a ballroom. He wondered about the gatherings that took place in that area. Suddenly, a shout startled him and froze him in his tracks.

"WHO IS THERE?" demanded Fermín.

"It's me, Martina." The maid replied nervously in a squeaky voice. "I am checking all doors before I retire for the evening."

"Who wants to see Don Julio?" demanded the man form a distance, "The guards told me that a young man was granted permission to come in."

"I haven't seen anybody. Do you want me to go and ask Señora?" replied the girl trying to avoid his eyes.

"Go to your sleeping quarters. I'll take over!" he commanded.

She turned to Leonardo before leaving, but he wasn't there. He had gone into the ballroom and found his way out through a window. Fermín checked every room and corner wishing the intruder was Leonardo. Just then, he noticed an open window in the ballroom. Now he knew exactly what to do.

Outside, Leonardo kept on looking back as he rushed to the main gate. The guards stopped him and asked if he had seen Fermín because the man had rushed in as soon as he had learned a young man had gone into the main quarters. After affirming that he wasn't needed anymore, he was cleared. His fast steps were only sufficient enough to get him to the main trail out to the stables. Once there, he began to run, trying not to trip or land in a hole. Rushing in the dark, he quickly got to the corral and the horse stables. He spotted the vet's home in the dim light just ahead of him. He found Arnulfo's men still tending the horses, and he was glad to stop and catch his breath. Miguel recognized him from far away. He signaled for him to come and join them to brush a brown colt.

"I haven't seen you the whole day. Have you kept yourself out of trouble?" he asked sarcastically.

"I've been around. I am helping with inventory at the storage house," replied Leonardo.

"My father told me. He is waiting for you inside the house, but before you go, let me introduce you to a future legend," insisted Miguel.

"This baby will take first place next week," he said patting the beast's forehead.

"Quite a beauty! Is it a thoroughbred? the Vallejo kid asked grabbing the horse's mane. "By the way, have you been as kind to my horse as you are to all these?"

"Oh yeah! One hundred percent purebred! Mmm, about your horse...let me think...I believe we sent him to the yoke team," replied the vet's son laughing.

"No way! Where is he?" asked Leonardo looking around the stable for the white stallion.

He was pacified to see him in the last stall impatiently roaming from side to side.

"You'd better brush him too. It is Beatriz' horse and he deserves the best care in the Hacienda. So, is my dinner ready?"

"What dinner?" inquired Miguel with a perplexed look.

"I lasted more than six seconds my friend. You lost the bet," affirmed Leonardo.

"But I just said it to challenge you. Are you going to hold me to my word?" protested the vet's son.

"We become men of honor when we keep our word," said Leonardo. "Alright, I'll give you a break. I will brush my horse, but you go and fix me a snack."

In a moment, Leonardo was the only one in the stables, glad to spend time with his best friend.

As he commenced to brush the animal, the barking of dogs jolted him. It was Fermín with fury in his eyes.

"What were you doing in Don Julio's quarters?" questioned the man accompanied by three armed men.

"Search him! Two of you go and search his belongings inside the house!"

Leonardo lifted his arms and affirmed that he didn't have anything nor did anything wrong while a man checked him. Right away, Arnulfo, who heard the noise, came out and confronted Fermín and his men.

"Leave him alone Fermín! Don't you see that he is finishing his last assignment for the day?

Look at the horses! All clean and brushed. He needs to finish the last one, especially that last one!"

Fermín took a good look at all the horses and wondered how long it would have taken to do all of them. He figured that maybe this time he was mistaken about the young man. His men came out of the house empty-handed, thus confirming Leonardo's innocence.

"Did you see anyone come from the main quarters through here?" asked Fermín.

"People come and go through here all the time. Who are you looking for? Has something been stolen?" inquired the vet.

"I don't know yet, but this week we go wolf hunting. I have a feeling we will slay many wolves!"

Fermín realized that his main responsibility was to guard the main quarters. He motioned to his men to go back and disappeared in the dark without a word. Arnulfo and Leonardo walked into the house glad to see them go away. Once inside, Miguel met them and called Leonardo to the room. He was embarrassed to admit that he was serving Leonardo. A delicious meal had been prepared by his sister Elena. The Vallejo kid even had enough food left for the next day's meal.

The Subintendent as Regidor

Meanwhile in Guanajuato, Don Julio got acquainted with Cirilo Del Castillo and his family. They had attended a long show at the opera house and had a great conversation during dinner. Two of the other area hacendados also brought taxes and gifts for the Regidor. Everything was ready for the next day's trip to Don Julio's estate.

That night as the boss lay in bed, he could not help to think about Cirilo's comments concerning a conspiracy to overthrow the vice royalty. He had resolved to deter any uprising at his own hacienda. He would invite the militia to showcase around his property and to strengthen his men. Now, his main concern had turned to Leonardo. The Regidor had asked him for a thorny favor that needed all his effort. Don Julio learned that Leonardo's father Joaquin and Don Cirilo had attended the same military college in Spain. They had been close friends, but military assignments had pulled them apart. Don Julio quickly gave an embellished account about Joaquin's unfortunate fate. His fake grief depicted a close relationship between the two. It was then that Cirilo had asked if there were any immediate family members left behind. He had a medal of honor to present to the family. Don Julio quickly suggested that it should be presented to Joaquin's brother Antonio. He cynically explained why Antonio was the lawful heir to the Vallejo bad credit and debts. He also made a full commitment to find out if there were any direct descendants in the area. Somehow, he felt that Cirilo knew about the Mestizo son. He knew that it was just a matter of time for the Regidor to start investigating Joaquin's assets.

"Should I hide the Vallejo kid or bring him to the Regidor? Oh no! That will bring questions about his father's belongings. But there is nothing to hide! Antonio is the legal proprietor and he probably sold the property by now! So far, I have nothing to do with that! On the other hand, if I reveal Leonardo as the sole Vallejo survivor in New Spain and act as his guardian, the Regidor will applaud my good heart for taking him in. Yes! I should do that. I need to talk to the young man as soon as possible."

The next morning, a caravan of six stagecoaches waited in front of the granite mansion. Cirilo's men had just finished loading the three cargo carriages when the Regidor's family came out to board. Don Julio accompanied the Regidor and his family in the first carriage. The other Hacendados followed in the second vehicle. The other carriage was for service people and luggage. An escort of thirty soldiers on cavalry also followed closely. Cirilo's jaripeo team already waited in the outer west side of town. They were supervised by his son Santiago who made sure that all the right horses and men were set for the trip and competition.

Before leaving town, one stop had to be made about two miles from Cirilo's mansion. Right in the middle of the city, there was a solid building that served as storage for the Crown. The Alhóndiga, as it was called, was a fort where ammunition, grain, and the army's supplies were kept and sold. Part of the extracted silver was packed in bars ready for shipment there. It was the most secure place in the land. Cirilo had to document his trip outside of the city and notify the Quartermaster Juan Antonio de Riaño. After twenty minutes, the company was on its way to a week long celebration at Don Julio's quarters.

Meanwhile at the Cortez Estate, Fermin meticulously checked every station and transaction in the storage houses. He also supervised the cleaning and decorations around the dusty trails near the structures. People from all over came to buy and sell produce and livestock. Leonardo had come early to the storehouse to try to finish the last three corn bags, but to his surprise, a fifty bag load came in shortly after. It was already noon, and it didn't look like he was going to finish. He had been assigned to go to the market after finishing that load. As he sweated lifting a sack to the balance, a familiar face came into the room. It was Mariano from the blacksmith shop. He came every year to assist in the market. He had been assigned to help him at his station.

"Mariano, over here!" called Leonardo when he saw him. Both rushed to shake hands and welcome their reunion.

"I knew that as soon as you got here, Don Julio would put you to work just like any of us. How are you besides working like a mule? Is the medicine career going well?" inquired Mariano.

"I am fine. I have learned a little bit more in the stables. I just need to be here for a while, but after the big fiesta my plans will change," responded Leonardo.

"I also have my own plans," added the blacksmith in a whispering tone.

The young men tackled the big loads and even sat together for lunch. The hard labor was more tolerable with friends around. Having a common oppressor helped them to become close friends in a short time.

By the end of the day, Leonardo was worried about Mariano's plans. He had told him about his hidden bayonet in a hollow tree.

"What will you do with it?" inquired Leonardo.

"You can see how unfair it is for us at the bottom! It chokes me to see Don Julio's face! But I have a big surprise for him during the jaripeo." Mariano whispered full of bitterness.

"Don't throw away your freedom by doing a foolish thing! Be careful!" The cowboy tried to dissuade him but was unsuccessful.

On his way to the stables, the fork in the road tempted Leonardo to continue towards the main quarters. He stood there in the dark, wrestling with his thoughts. He was abruptly awakened by a slow cart, full of corn stalks, which almost ran him over. It was a great hiding place to take him to the main house. After cautiously climbing aboard, he found out that it was full of jalapeños and tomatoes. The cart went through the back of the house directly to the kitchen. The area was well known by him now. He gently got off before the vehicle came to a full stop.

"Hey, what are you doing muchacho? Stay away from the cart!" shouted the man driving the team.

"I am here to help you unload! Do you want me to see if they are ready in the kitchen?" answered Leonardo.

"Who sent you here?"

"I know Martina is always busy making cheese at this time. I wanted to give her a break. Do you mind?" asked the young man.

"I see. So you are trying to impress her! You little fox! Give me a hand then," replied the man laughing.

Leonardo took a wooden box full of produce and entered the kitchen. He continued to make trips in and out until the wagon was unloaded. He bid farewell to the man and remained in the kitchen hoping for Martina come around. Suddenly, a man startled him as he glanced to the hallway from the kitchen.

"What are you doing? Who are you?"

"I delivered all the vegetables and fruit for tomorrow. I wanted to make sure someone was here to acknowledge it," answered the young cowboy.

"That would be the women who prepare the meals. They should be here soon. I bring the milk every morning, and once a week I get a little cheese. Stay around," waived the man leaving through the door that led to the garden.

Just then, Leonardo saw the two guards from the previous night on their way to the kitchen. He had no alternative than to walk through the corridor into the main quarters again. He passed by the stairs that were next to the large hall. He knew that it was his escape route, but voices from the library caught his attention.

"So you see! I have access to any place in the mansion, I am second in command. The Spaniard trusts me even with his own life. He doesn't have a slightest idea about our plans. It's time for a new order of government and new people to be in control. We shouldn't be paying taxes to a distant king. Out with the Spanish gachupines! We the Creoles are the rightful heirs to the land. Remember, the last day of the jaripeo you will be serving in here. We will strike on that night," a man explained.

Leonardo recognized the voice and hid by the doorway that led to the ballroom. He wanted to see their faces, but it was too risky after what he heard. Again, he had no other choice than to exit the same way he did the previous night. This time, he knew the guards were in the kitchen.

"Who would have thought that Fermín would be fighting for the right cause? No, no way! That snake has his own bloody agenda. He will take every opportunity to seize control. His thirst for more power will demolish anyone in his way. I need to tell Beatriz and Don Julio," Leonardo worried.

He spent part of the night tossing and turning, studying the situation. Once the rooster's cry announced a new day, he left directly to the storehouse.

"Fermín is waiting for you in the market place!" the administrator shouted.

"Fermín? Do you know what he wants?" Leonardo asked.

"You will find out when you get there. Go!" commanded the man.

From far, Leonardo distinguished Fermín biting a guava and talking to the man in charge of currency. The expression on his face convinced everyone to keep away.

"Here! Come this way! You will help here until I say otherwise!" shouted the second in command when he saw the young cowboy, "You will help with the sales in produce."

At the main quarters, Beatriz and her mother nervously checked every detail in preparation for the Castillo Family stay. They would be arriving at any moment. They had new flowers in every vase and clean linen in every room. Beatriz was annoyed by her mother's repetitive discourse about Santiago Del Castillo's talents. She already knew that her father and mother were more interested in his wealth rather than her happiness.

"I can't stand this anymore! I'm afraid I will go mad! If I could only disappear for this week, but I promised my father I would try. There is no way to avoid the situation. I must try to make the best of it."

Before noon, she had an idea. She immediately went to her mother and told her.

"Mother, I am very nervous about the parade ride. I need to practice it one last time," Beatriz begged.

"What do you mean you are not ready? Your father told me you were. There is no time for practice. They will be here at any moment!" her mother replied in a worried tone.

"No! I am not ready and I need to rehearse the last lap with Leonardo."

"Leonardo! Leonardo! You are talking about him all the time. I need to meet this Leonardo!"

"You will. I can ask him to come right after we finish," suggested the girl.

"Do it fast, and let Fermín know so he can send a guard with you. Martina! Martina! Go with Beatriz to the stables," ordered Don Julio's wife.

Beatriz was very excited to be on her way to see Leonardo. She had thought about him the whole day. She never told Fermín of her whereabouts, but one of the guards accompanied them all the way to the corral near the stables. Just then, she remembered that Leonardo wasn't there. She sent her maid and the guard to find him at the storage rooms. She continued walking to the stables to get her horse ready. When Miguel saw her coming, he immediately rushed to Lightning's stall. He wanted to make sure the stallion was brushed and clean before she rode him. As Beatriz walked towards the white horse, an attractive Elena came across with a covered basket. She bowed but did not stray from her errand. Beatriz felt uneasy about the look on Elena's face but just stared at her as she walked away.

After a moment, the horse was saddled and ready to be ridden. She was getting impatient because there was no sign of Leonardo on the walkway. She pulled the horse's rope and walked to the corral. At a distance, she noticed her messengers coming back without Leonardo. She left the horse and advanced to confront them.

"Where is Leonardo?" she demanded.

"He is not at the storeroom. He has been assigned to the market. The supervisor will not release him unless Fermín approves," replied Martina looking back at the guard.

"Let's see what he says when I tell him off face to face," challenged the young woman turning on her way to the storage rooms. Her fast paces revealed her determination.

Meanwhile, it was a loud scene at the market place. Leonardo was assigned to oversee the sale of produce which included weighing and accounting for the cash received. People from around the area sold their harvest and exchanged their earnings for goods. Many poor farmers were afraid to complain about the high cost of provisions. The Vallejo young man had been working nonstop since the morning. He couldn't wait for the afternoon recess. It was one hour past noon when the whistle blew. Everyone stopped to rest, and more importantly, to catch a meal. From the crowd someone waved and called Leonardo's name. It was Elena inviting him to come. He was surprised to see her there and quickly noticed she had food for him. As he approached her, she looked at him with tender eyes. He couldn't deny her pleasant smile.

"I am grateful to see what you do for me," said Leonardo.

"You have become one of us, and we need to look out for each other," replied the young woman leading him towards the big tree where many sat. She extended a blanket on the grass and prepared to have a personal picnic among tens of people. Leonardo sat down trying to quiet down his growling stomach. The men from the day before greeted him and acknowledged his luck when they passed by. Most workers were aware that someday, a fortunate young man would be permitted to court the horse whisperer's daughter. They assumed today was the day.

"Your father has done so much for me. I don't know how I can pay him back."

"Don't worry about that. He values your friendship very much. You already have done so much by preparing the white colt and assisting Señorita Beatriz. That has taken a big load off my father's back."

"How did you know I was in the market place?" he asked.

"I went to see the administrator, and he told me you weren't there but Mariano; I believe he worked with you yesterday, told me you had been reassigned," she continued, "I remember him from last year, but I haven't seen him around. Where is he from?"

"He is from the blacksmith shop in Teocaltiche. Don Julio assigns him to come and help at this time every year. He is very capable. I can introduce him to you if you want to meet him?"

"Oh no, I was just curious about his origin," she answered with little discomfort on her face.

"Are you excited about the jaripeo? How do you think your father's team will do?"

"I can't wait, but I am very nervous about the big race! My father tries so hard, I wish we could get second place. That would be sufficient for me!" Elena replied.

"Second? Why not first?" he asked surprised by her comment.

"The Guanajuato racers are invincible, we have tried many times, but we always come too short."

"Your brother Miguel assured me that his stallion will take first place. Have a little faith in him," he encouraged.

"I guess you are right, I am giving up too soon," she giggled.

Leonardo admired Elena's friendly nature and her freedom to go and come around the Hacienda.

From a distance, two beautiful black eyes couldn't believe what they were seeing. It was Beatriz standing in the middle of the road battling a jab of jealousy. Her thoughts betrayed her.

"How can Leonardo be with another woman? Is he trying to ridicule me?"

It was public knowledge, and she was the last one to find out. She stared intensely, hoping to be mistaken, but it was him. She thought about confronting them, but that act would have made her emotions too obvious. She would not accept that a girl like herself, the very Hacendado's daughter, could come down and start a quarrel for a servant, who was flirting with another servant. With a hurt pride, she turned around and left the scene. Tender tears mixed with anger rolled down her cheeks. Her maid witnessed her disappointment as she followed closely back home.

"How could I have been so blind? I trusted him! Oh Martina! I fell for it! I am the trustee's daughter! I own everything here! How can a woman of my class waste her time with a peasant like Leonardo? I was so foolish! But I'm not going to leave it like that! He will pay for all his lies. They continued in a fast pace when Fermín intercepted them on their way to the main quarters.

"I was told that you needed to practice one last time. Do you really need Leonardo to help you? Can't some other cowboy help you?" he complained.

"Don't worry, I can do it by myself," she replied making a sudden turn towards the stables.

"You can keep him forever if you want."

"I am glad to hear that. We need all the help we can get! I was beginning to think you were giving him special privileges. He will be in the storage room until the last day of the Jaripeo," announced the man in a suspicious tone.

She went directly to the stables and rode by herself all the way to the lagoon. The guard and Martina followed but never caught up to her.

Meanwhile, Leonardo said goodbye to his sweet acquaintance and returned to work. Fermín thought that produce was a light assignment for Leonardo, so he sent him back to the storage room with Mariano.

Leonardo worried when Fermín approached his stand. He remembered about the incident of the previous night and the disturbing plans to overthrow the Hacendado. His anxiety dispelled when the man commanded him to go back to work at the storage place. Mariano was delighted to see him back. As soon as they were alone, he began teasing and inquiring about his love adventure.

"You sure don't lose any time. Even in this slave condition, love follows you around."

"What do you mean?" asked Leonardo.

"You sound very convincing when you say that you will become a doctor someday. I honestly don't think Don Julio will let you. Is that what you tell all the girls to get them interested in you?" alleged the blacksmith.

"I still don't know what you mean, but Don Julio cannot stop me because he doesn't own me! I will be a doctor. I don't have any doubt about my direction in life! I will do it. It is a good thing, a great thing! Who will oppose? It's all about believing in oneself! People who doubt their objectives will hardly accomplish them," Leonardo lectured.

"How can we accomplish any objectives if we are oppressed?" posed Mariano.

"Exactly! That's the first objective, overcoming oppression! Workers need to demand limits on excessive work hours. Do you understand it? The first and real revolution to be won is in people's minds. We have to liberate ourselves from low expectations, self pity, and binding old ways!" stated the cowboy. "Have you taken the time to think where you will be in ten years?"

"You are so blind! Where have you been? You know that we are deprived from our rights by force and intimidation! Who will teach us the alphabet if we can't afford to pay? And even if they try, we can't learn to read when our kids are starving to death, and a rifle's barrel is pointing to our face! We work like mules! Look around! Most of this food will rot while people's bellies are empty. The only way to set our limits ourselves is by eliminating the oppressor. We must own the land and grow our own food! The land belongs to us, but they have stolen it! Can't you see that? Don't be mistaken, I know where I will be in ten years. Either free from slavery or stiff underground," countered Mariano.

"You are right Mariano, there is a great injustice in the distribution of property and the chances for learning. I should not be judging you when I know I had everything as a child. But still, I should become a doctor! I will be in a better position to help then! Be careful with what you say and do. Not all Spaniards think or act the way you say."

"You go ahead with your plans, and I'll take the real front," said the blacksmith.

"Revolution needs all fronts. I will be doing my part."

"That's the easy part!" muttered the blacksmith.

"A university study is hard work! The sleepless nights are mandatory not a choice! What do you mean with your comments that love follows me around?" asked Leonardo.

"You know exactly what I mean. I am talking about the sweet lady who brought you a meal and the second one who came asking for you. She said that Don Julio's daughter needed your services at the stables."

"Why didn't you tell me earlier? That must have been Martina, Beatriz' maid," protested Leonardo.

"And who is Beatriz?" asked Mariano.

"She is Don Julio's daughter. She is the most important woman in my life at this time."

"Don't be a fool! Are you falling for a woman like that? She will never set her eyes on you!"

"Keep her out of your revenge! She is in my plans," warned the cowboy defensively.

Mariano remained silent and surprised at his reaction. He now knew that she could be a great target for his revenge. He had realized that he could make Beatriz pay for his sister's miseries. Leonardo left the station and went looking for the supervisor. He was happy to know that

Beatriz wanted to see him. The supervisor quickly assured him that his assignment was at the storage house and that no one had changed his task. He was then escorted back to his post.

"Are you telling the truth? Somebody came looking for me?" Leonardo asked Mariano in a desperate tone.

"Yes! A girl from the main quarters came looking for you right after you left for lunch!" confirmed the blacksmith.

"What did she look like?"

"She was an Indian maid with long braids."

"It was definitively Beatriz' servant. I need to find out what's going on!" Leonardo concluded.

"My friend, you are not leaving me with all this work. You and I have this huge pile to tackle!"

Leonardo had no choice but to stay and grapple with the assignment and the thoughts in his head.

Back home, Beatriz felt heart-broken. To avoid being seen so disheartened, she went straight to her chamber. The sound of barking dogs and annoyed turkeys signaled visitors approaching the Hacienda. It was Don Julio and Cirilo Del Castillo with company. Several servants who moved like an assembly line greeted them and carried their baggage to different guestrooms in the house. Once the Regidor crossed under the brick arch entrance, a sound of trumpets announced Royal representation in the quarters. It also signaled the jaripeo kick off event the next day. Santiago Del Castillo, the Regidor's son, was disposed to meet the horse whisperer in the Hacienda. He wanted to know who would be responsible for his animals. He commissioned his horse tender and his men to bring all his pure blood stallions and personally secured stalls in the stables. They were to lodge and watch over the horses. Santiago was tired from the trip and desired to rest. He wasn't too happy to be away from the city for so many days, but it was true that he was a little excited to be competing in the last event of the celebration.

"Why does it have to be the last event and not the first one?" He lamented.

A formal reception had been planned to honor the Castillo Family that evening. Don Julio already felt the pressure. The following days needed to go exactly as planned. They would mark a decisive turn in his life. He sent for Fermín and the supervisor to make sure they were ready to receive and host the other Hacendados. He also wanted the small cavalry of soldiers allocated in key places during the celebration. Right away, he went to see Beatriz to confirm she knew they were home. He worried about her reaction to his plans. He found her still in riding outfit and unmindful to what was happening downstairs.

"My princess, why aren't you with your mother greeting our distinguished guests?" he asked.

"Oh my father, I needed you so much! I wasn't aware that you were here already," she replied running to embrace him.

"Do you know that we will have a reception for the Castillos at supper time? You need to look gorgeous! I know you are already, but you need to wear your best attire," he suggested.

That evening, El Camino Real was busier than ever before. Carts and carriages full of people and goods kept arriving. A full orchestra, a marching band, and hosts of people from all over the region reached the location. It was the merriest place in the land. Inside the hacienda, the aristocracy carried out its role of looking better than the next person. Hosts and guests wore elegant clothing and eagerly recited their family tree to attest lawful noble ancestry.

As soon as the orchestra was put in place, a marching melody encumbered the ballroom. It was a formal announcement for everyone to stand. The people needed to acknowledge Don Cirilo Del Castillo and his family as they entered the room. They were accompanied by Don Julio and his wife, but there was no sign of Beatriz. The crowd clapped the same way they do when royalty walks on the red carpet. Some people quickly turned to their neighbor and criticized the women's gowns and latest fashion. The main table was right across the main entrance. Once everyone sat down, a succulent dinner was served.

Don Julio and his wife sent for Beatriz; they knew how important her presence was at the reception. Right in that moment, her stunning beauty caught everyone's attention when she entered the ballroom. She commenced by waving to Estela her best friend. All present recognized that Don Julio's daughter was the most attractive woman in the house. The main table seemed to be leagues away from Beatriz' firm steps on the marble floor. Santiago looked intensely as she walked across the room to the table. His thoughts almost became transparent.

"Oh yes! This visit here will not be as bad as I thought! I have to meet this woman."

Don Julio proudly stood to introduce his daughter to everyone at his table. Santiago couldn't wait to meet her and kiss her hand. Beatriz was nervous; the idea that she was meeting her future husband felt like trying to remember an abstract dream.

"Santiago Del Castillo, it is indeed a pleasure to meet you," said the twenty five year old bachelor when Beatriz extended her hand and fixed her eyes on him for the first time.

She thought of saying the pleasure is mine, but she just smiled and nodded affirmatively to continue meeting the rest of the family. A seat was reserved for her right across the Regidor's son. She began to feel uneasy because not only Santiago stared at her, but all the other girls in the room. They inwardly resented not sitting at that table. Don Julio did not hesitate to say accolades about his daughter, but they weren't necessary…the bachelor was already interested in her.

"I understand you will leave for Madrid to complete your schooling, is that so?" asked Santiago looking directly at Beatriz.

"She will leave right after this Christmas," replied Don Julio. He quickly noticed that his response annoyed Santiago who wanted to start a conversation with Beatriz.

"What course of study will you pursue once in the university?" Santiago continued.

"I will be studying administration, but I'm also interested in human behavior and history," replied Beatriz speaking for the first time at the table.

She wanted to know Santiago's views on the government and the role of women, but that was a men only conversation. She also needed to find out what he thought about marriage without sounding suggestive.

"What was the most important lesson for your life in all your studies?" she asked.

Santiago was amazed by such a pondering question and took a moment to answer. Everyone at the table was also surprised at her words and became eager to hear his response.

"I will say that it wasn't a single lesson but an accumulation of philosophies that help me see the world in a deeper way. I can make my own conclusions," he answered.

"And those conclusions are?" she continued.

"I believe that a man has to be able to manage his family assets to make his own fortune first. Then, find his place among the elite. Finally, he needs to settle down after he finds a good woman to marry. Is that the response you were looking for?" he asked.

"That's good enough for today," she replied.

As they savored the delicious meal, a toast was proposed on behalf of the people present.

Right after the toast, the orchestra played a romantic melody for couples to join on the dance floor. In a rush, Santiago stood up to ask Beatriz to dance but when he tried to go around the table, a good-looking woman blocked his way. It was Estela. She had been bold enough to take him to the middle of the dance floor. As they danced, Santiago continued looking at Beatriz. It was a planned move because Eleodoro came and invited Beatriz to dance.

The floor was quickly filled with people enjoying the music and performing a routine choreography. Eleodoro had slyly requested the orchestra to play that specific piece of music because it had a long decrescendo waltz which permitted the couple to dance alone. He thought it would be the perfect time to express his affection for Beatriz.

"Beatriz, I know you are leaving in three months and I am aware that there is a possibility you might not come back. That will make everyone sad, especially me! If you want to stay, I can have my father talk to your father. I can also follow you to Madrid if you wish. Don't say a word! I want you to think about my proposal and where I am going with this," declared the bold young man.

Before she could say a word, the music pattern changed, and it was time to break away and face other dancers. Don Julio watched desperately and felt uneasy about Beatriz' partner. He did not know how to get Santiago and his daughter together. The new piece of music seemed to go on forever, but it was working to Don Julio's benefit. Santiago was longing to be with Beatriz again. Out of courtesy, he faked to be enjoying Estela's company.

There was no one to stand in Don Julio's way to keep him from his objective. Showing that he was the boss, the Hacendado commanded the orchestra to stop the song. He called everyone's attention and made an announcement.

"Good evening! Please excuse the interruption! I am Don Julio Cortez, the Hacendado in this region. Welcome to my home. I hope everyone enjoyed dinner and continues to celebrate all night if necessary. Of course, I am exaggerating! What I really mean is that you will need your energies because this celebration continues for the whole week! We are honored to have the Regidor, Don Cirilo Del Castillo and his family among us. Welcome to New Spain! We congratulate you on your achievements! Your new assignment is very significant. Such a responsibility cannot be trusted to just anybody, and we know you are the right person for this position. At this time, I am equally delighted to introduce your son Santiago Del Castillo, a great young man who already graduated from the university in Vienna. He is a talented man with a wonderful future! I heard that he will be competing in the race on Friday. I am rooting for you already! I am putting my name on the line for your team! Before we continue with our celebration and to honor our prominent guest, my daughter Beatriz will perform a selected piece of music with her violin."

By this time, Beatriz was standing next to Estela, trying to be unnoticed. She wasn't surprised by her father's words. He did that at every social gathering. She was so familiar with the song that she didn't use her music sheet anymore.

"Here we go again!" said Estela, "Play something new this time."

"It is new for the Castillos," replied Beatriz.

Santiago was thrilled to learn that she was fond of music. He had majored in piano and sometimes wrote his own compositions. He listened intensively as she played, without losing sight of her throughout the song. Almost next to him, someone else sighed with the melody. Eleodoro hoped she would reciprocate his feelings. He was also ready to win the race, not only the race to win her heart, but also the race on Friday. Beatriz excelled at the violin. She performed to impress and impress she did.

As soon as the clapping and praising faded away, Santiago moved through the crowd and took her by the hand. He then signaled the musicians to commence playing the next piece. Beatriz felt flattered as he complemented her talent. She couldn't deny that her earlier melancholy was placed in the back of her heart. She was nervous because he was holding her hand, and his green eyes looked intently at her countenance.

"Maybe my parents are right. This man could be the man of my dreams! I need to get to know him better in the following days to confirm it." Breatiz thought.

She also remembered Eleodoro's pleas and felt privileged for such possibilities.

After a while, the people began to retire. A selected group of men went ahead into Don Julio's library to discuss politics and to get better acquainted. Among them were the five Hacendados and the Regidor. The central topic was the government's volatile condition.

"Gentlemen! We need to be united more than ever. We are so much alike. We are stewards for our mother country, we all function as governors in the estate, and we are all loyal to our superiors. The Crown has all confidence in you. We must join against insurgents! We have discovered a clandestine movement to overthrow the government. We are struggling to identify them because they are within the army officials, the clergy, and influential Creoles. Let's be aware and serious about rebel groups in this area. Can you believe that some priests turned against the church and the Vice-royalty? Do not hesitate to bring them to justice. We used the firing squad out in public last week in Guanajuato. It is a real way to deter further traitors. The conspirators we executed last week refused to give us names," the Regidor explained.

The party continued their discussion about loyalty and economic rewards among the estates. Cirilo del Castillo's greater fear was to see any of the five change allegiance.

In Beatriz's chamber, a more positive topic materialized. Their laughter could be heard out the window.

"Why didn't you tell me about your brother Eleodoro?" demanded Beatriz.

"I knew you would hold it against me, but I had promised him I wouldn't tell you," answered Estela. "He's had a big crush on you for a long time. He wasn't brave enough to tell you. But imagine if you become my sister in law, you can't go wrong with this family!"

"Oh, I am in a difficult situation! I need time to think about it."

"You really need is to listen to your heart. I can understand if you choose Santiago over my brother. If that is the case, I would respect it," commented Estela.

"Let's talk about Santiago. He is handsome, sure of himself, plus he is a total gentleman!" boasted Beatriz.

"I think you like him, and I think he likes you too."

"What makes you say that?" asked Beatriz.

"He couldn't keep his eyes away from you when I was dancing with him. He even asked me if I knew you well," replied Estela.

"Wait, I think he is trying to make new friends. He is also aware that I am the Hacendado's daughter, so he is trying to be polite."

"Come on! Didn't you notice when he was dancing with you? He was melting away. He accompanied you out of the ballroom, all the way to the stairs! Girl, you have him in the palm of your hands."

"You are jumping to conclusions," said Beatriz.

Meanwhile, there was another atmosphere surrounding the stables. Some provisional tents were set in front of the stalls. The racers did not rely on local horse tenders. They wanted to guard their own animals day and night just in case someone tried something illegal. In previous years, there had been some arguments and accusations about contaminated food for the stallions. Ever since, riders brought their own provisions to the competition.

After long hours of hard work, the marketplace finally closed. Leonardo and Mariano felt relief because they had just finished putting the left over produce in place. It was their last assignment before they could go home for the day. The news of the Regidor's presence at the main quarters had reached them. Leonardo had already decided to go and see Don Julio, and of course, to find out how Beatriz was doing. Right after he was dismissed by the supervisor, Fermín called him to the door.

"Since Señorita Beatriz doesn't need you anymore, tomorrow you will leave the Hacienda! You will accompany a group of cowboys to round up the wild herd. All of our trading horses are sold out, but we still have some unfinished business to resolve. Arnulfo will lead the expedition, you will return in three days."

Leonardo did not like the new assignment at all. He knew that this new task would take him far from the girl he already missed. Nonetheless, after pondering it for a moment, he realized that it would give him a great opportunity to sneak out and see Beatriz. After all, he would be under Arnulfo's commands. He was less harsh and more understanding with him. He also concluded that his initial agreement in coming to the Cieneguilla was to learn from the vet.

"That's fine with me, but I need to talk to Don Julio as soon as possible. Can you take me to him?" Leonardo asked.

"Not right now. He is busy with very important people. Why do you need to see him with such urgency anyway? Are you questioning my orders again?" Fermín confronted.

"You can keep your authority. No one can dispute it. It's about the promise he made to my father and me before coming here."

"Who is your father?"

Leonardo looked at him and hesitated to answer, but Fermín demanded to know.

"My father was Joaquin Vallejo."

That name struck a bell in his ears. He couldn't believe what the young cowboy was saying.

"Do you mean, Major Joaquin Vallejo?" Fermín asked feeling a little nervous.

"Yes. How do you know my father?"

"I...I accompanied Don Julio to La Casa Grande a few times when they met. Now, go home and get ready for tomorrow morning."

Leonardo was intrigued by his reaction. For a moment, he considered the possibility that his father and Fermín had secretly agreed to change the system together; however, he was seriously concerned about Fermín's conspiracy to eliminate Don Julio.

"Which side is he on? My father would have told me about him when he spoke about Allende and Aldama's plans," he thought as he walked to the stables.

Fermín remained thinking about the young man's true origin. He became interested in knowing why Don Julio had brought him over.

"Why does the boss treat him like a servant? This kid is loaded with silver. Wait a minute! Can this be a trick to find out what really happened to his father?" he conjectured, "Maybe the keen Hacendado took the spoil. Does the kid know anything about the wealth his father left behind? I'd better find out! I will keep Leonardo away from the boss while I find more rope to cut."

By this time, Leonardo felt upset because it was too late to visit Beatriz. He was also feeling disappointed about missing the Jaripeo inauguration, especially Beatriz' inaugural ride. He continued directly towards the corral, but as he got closer, he was surprised to see so many people at the stables. He hurried to confirm his horse was there. He walked around the temporary settlements until he reached Lightning's place. The stallion immediately recognized him and shook his mane when he touched it. Leonardo knew he could not take the colt on the round up because the horse would be part of the family parade the next day. Miguel and his team were there also watching over the horses. After making sure his animal would be fine for the next several days, he went straight to see the horse whisperer. He found him cleaning a rifle and preparing for the trip to the Alamito Valley where most of the herd grazed.

"You know we leave at five in the morning, so find a canteen and a good horse. We will be back in three days if everything goes well," announced the vet.

"Do you really need me to go?" Leonardo complained.

"Do you prefer to stay and break your back at the storehouse? You have to be kidding me! I had to quarrel with the administrator for an hour before he consented to let you come. I need at least ten people, people who I can depend on. Leading and rounding wild horses for such a long distance is a day and night shift! You might be right; it's much easier to stay here. For your information, this is a direct order from the top. I included you on the expedition to get you away from Fermín. He is acting suspicious lately. I don't have a good feeling about him. Besides, we need fifty additional beasts to supply the army. I believe Don Julio offered them to the soldiers in exchange for protection," explained Arnulfo.

"I will see Don Julio as soon as we get back. It's time to return back home to La Casa Grande," Leonardo said with resentment, "I am certain that I've been fooled by Don Julio, and it's time for me to do something about it!"

"So what are you going to do?" asked Arnulfo.

"I will find the proper documentation about my father's will and assets. I will travel to the Capital City if needed. I will hire a lawyer and seek audience with the Vice-Royalty if necessary! I do not trust Don Julio anymore. I need to find out if he is telling the truth!"

"Without money, I don't think you will get very far. It is too late to see Don Julio right now, and there is no way to see him tomorrow. Your best bet is to seek out the Regidor now that he is here," advised the vet.

Leonardo knew he could trust Arnulfo. Maybe it was a good time to open up to him, and hear what he thought about Beatriz and him. He would have plenty of time during the trip.

In the main quarters, everyone was sleeping except for Beatriz. She was surrounded by so many people, but at the end of the day, she felt lonely. It had been a day full of new experiences and people, but a single image was wedged like a thorn in her heart. Her pillow was wet as she pondered about her very possible arranged marriage. Suddenly, her thoughts were interrupted when she remembered Leonardo and Elena. She still had a tiny hope that all was a misunderstanding; therefore, she decided to go see him in the morning.

Although the Jaripeo started at three o'clock, people always arrived two hours early. They wanted to secure a good seat and shop around the market place. In the rodeo arena, the main lower section was reserved for aristocracy. Their rows were decorated with red ribbons and a blue roof tarp to provide distinction, shade, and comfort.

During the opening, Don Julio, his wife, and Beatriz would ride around the arena to greet and welcome their friends. Their Jaripeo team would follow them to showcase their horses and to hold the welcoming banner. The first events after the inauguration would be bull riding and horse breaking. More competition of lassoing, bronco-riding, calf-roping, and steer-wrangling would be displayed the following day. A horse jumping exhibition and the ring race were scheduled for the third day.

Beatriz woke up early. She went to the kitchen and exited through the side door. Martina came along and both continued on the way to the main crossway. In a few minutes, they arrived at the storage place. Beatriz' heart beat faster as she hurried to see Leonardo. They passed the room and continued on to the market place. Since they could not find him there, they decided to go back to the storage room and ask the administrator. Beatriz waited outside while her maid inquired about him.

"He is not here! He doesn't work here anymore!" the man explained, "The last thing I heard was that he had left the Hacienda!"

Astonished at the news, Beatriz began to walk away without wanting to hear another word.

"He left because he didn't want to confront me? That confirms his dishonesty!" she concluded.

Martina remained behind and continued inquiring about the cowboy.

"When did he leave? Why? Who sent him away?"

"He is on his way to the Alamito Valley. I believe Arnulfo is leading an expedition there to round up horses. They left early this morning," he answered, "Don Julio ordered it!"

"When will they be back?" she asked.

"In three days if they're lucky. It is a dangerous trail. Horse thieves infest the canyons and rebel forces recruit in that area," he replied.

By the time he finished explaining, Beatriz was far from them. She was annoyed not only by the news, but also by the big tree where she saw Leonardo for the last time. Her heart felt defeated, and her tangled thoughts didn't help a bit.

"I should've come sooner and stopped him! Now I will never know the truth. But what if there is a good reason for his actions? Maybe he thought I was unreachable, that's why he chose Elena. He has no excuse! He doesn't deserve my time."

Martina ran after her, but Beatriz was rushing home. She finally caught up to her by the crossroads. Beatriz debated about going to Elena's house to confront her; she then realized it would be foolish. She turned to her maid and ordered her to go. Martina was to find out what had happened between Leonardo and the horse whisperer's daughter.

"He is helping Arnulfo's men to round up wild horses. He will be back in three days," the maid explained trying to appease Beatriz.

"Also, find out if he has taken my horse! I will see you in the kitchen after breakfast," commanded Beatriz.

Breakfast was served late that morning. Everyone was already seated when she entered the house. Sneaking through another door, she went to her chamber to freshen up her face. When she came down, Beatriz noticed that her father had arranged a seat for her across Santiago. The bachelor's eyes were fixed on her when she joined them at the table. He was pleased to see her and praised her looks.

"So I hear that you are an excellent rider!" he said.

"Whoever told you that is exaggerating! I only ride one horse, and even then, someone has to pull the rope," she responded with a giggle.

"I would be glad to be that someone some time," he added.

She just smiled. She silently thought she already had someone.

"I assume you have a lot of experience with horses, do you?" she asked.

"I love horses. I grew up among them, and I think they are the smartest, kindest, and most useful animals in the world. They have been one of the best gifts Europe has given America," he explained.

"That is an interesting comment. We have heard a few folktales by the Mexican natives. They speak of using and admiring horses way back before Columbus. They were the original vaqueros. Have you heard anything about that?" Beatriz asked.

"No, that's new to me, but supposing that is true, I am positive Europe has the better breed."

"How would you react if you lost the race on Friday?" Beatriz insinuated.

He was startled by such a question. It sounded like a challenge.

"I don't know. I am a champion! I have never lost a single race in my life; neither in Europe or in New Spain. I think I can't be beaten," he bragged.

"There is always a first time. It could also be a turning point in your life."

"I am well aware that one day I will be too old to compete, but I will retire before I get close to being defeated. Not this Friday, no way!"

He looked at her intensely. She seemed more charming than the night before. Her comments and her intelligence impressed Santiago.

"Beatriz, what do you mean when you say that this race could be a turning point? Are you referring to the direction I am headed in life or just a lesson to be learned?" he asked.

"Santiago is ahead of his generation," interrupted Don Julio, "he grew up at the feet of great men like his own father. He has gained vast experience by observing his father. His intelligence and education makes him the most likely to succeed. Of course, he is headed in the right direction."

"Those are very kind words. I feel privileged and grateful for my good fortune," added the bachelor.

"There is only one important ingredient missing in my son's life," revealed the bachelor's father.

"And that ingredient is?" inquired Don Julio.

"A wife! My son needs to settle down and make his own way in life. With so many exceptional acquaintances, he can't make up his mind," the Regidor explained drinking from the glass.

"Will you cheer for me on Friday?" asked Santiago attempting to change the conversation.

"You put me in a difficult situation. I always side with my father. You are running against my father's team," replied Beatriz.

"This time, don't follow your heart darling, follow your brain. You have my permission to choose. Maybe sometime today, Santiago could show you his stallions and his strategy. You know about the quality of our colts and riders; cheer for the right one," stated Don Julio.

"Father, we cheer and encourage the ones who are dear to us. That's why I am on your side," she explained.

"My dear, during the big race, you have to cheer for the winner," Don Julio explained. "If you think we are the best, you are headed in the right direction. However, if Santiago convinces you that he is, then root for him. I am not offended, not a tiny bit."

"Do you want my son to show her around, so she can spy on us? Is that your strategy?" blurted Cirilo with a loud laughter.

"You and I are too proud to cheer for someone else. I am warning you, a whole year of annoyance awaits the loser. This year the prize stays here," challenged Don Julio.

The other Hacendados gained the courage to root for their estate after hearing Don Julio's audacious words. It was the spark that brought the competitiveness lacking so far in the celebration.

"I am going to take your father's offer. Can you show me around the Hacienda after breakfast?" asked Santiago looking at the girl.

Beatriz nodded being too shy to respond. Estela caught her eye and then looked at her brother who was almost dripping with jealousy. Eleodoro was not going to give up easily. Beatriz was the love of his life, and he was confident that his team would be victorious.

"This race will not only determine the best estate and the best trust, but it will also prove that the New World, America, has surpassed Europe in many areas," proudly announced Eleodoro.

"Now, that is a bold statement," exclaimed Don Julio.

"An understatement to be exact!" reacted Santiago trying to identify the challenger.

"If it pleases Beatriz and her parents, I propose that the winner should have the first dance with her at the ball on Friday," said Eleodoro.

"I'll be glad to dance with her," interrupted Santiago.

"I have a better idea. I will dance with the loser!" declared Beatriz with displeasure.

She disliked the idea of being used as a trophy. Don Julio remained quiet, it was evident that he wasn't pleased with either proposals.

After breakfast, everyone rushed to get ready for the kick off event. Santiago insisted on taking a walk with Beatriz. Don Julio encouraged them to go because he wanted to make sure his daughter corresponded like a first-class hostess. Eleodoro had a plan of his own. He had already told his sister to join them outside the Hacienda.

As soon as they walked out the main gate, Estela appeared from the side.

"Wait for me! I want to see your horses too!"

"Only if you join Beatriz and root for me," Santiago proposed.

They proceeded to the stables and got lost in the multitude of people already at the rodeo.

Fermín placed guards on the roof of every major structure. He had become acquainted with the lieutenant in charge of the small army. He even treated him to warm meals and beverages. His secret plans to strike on the last day of the celebration only needed execution. Arnulfo was away and maybe never to be back. That was the way Fermín had arranged it. His obsession to marry the Boss's daughter would be fulfilled once Don Julio was eliminated.

At the stables, Eleodoro was already putting down the Regidor's riders. He had rushed to the site to keep an eye on Don Julio's daughter. He took out his anger on the cowboys when he didn't find the couple. He tried to alarm the Regidor's riders, ensuring that he would win the race on Friday; however, the riders were not intimidated.

Back at the main quarters, the Hacendados were ready to walk on to the rodeo arena. Don Julio was furious because he had just learned that Arnulfo was away from the Hacienda. He sent for Fermín and Miguel, he wanted them his office at once.

"WHY WASN'T I INFORMED THAT ARNULFO WAS GONE? How in the world do you send the Jaripeo's key person away during the competition? I ordered you to go and bring the livestock yourself!" hollered Don Julio.

Fermín was more deeply hurt by his words than by the push on his shoulder. He thought he was the key person in the Hacienda.

"He does a lot better with horses. I have too many things to keep in order here," he muttered.

"That's out of the question! I needed him here during the race, and he is not, and only because you didn't use your brains!" fumed the Hacendado.

"I should have checked with you before sending him. It won't happen again. Please forgive me!" Fermín begged.

"Nothing is done without my consent! I need to be informed of everything! It is the last time you take matters in to your own hands! Is that understood?" railed the Boss. "When will he return?"

"In three days."

"Now, go back to the arena and secure a seat close to me! Make sure Miguel knows exactly what to do! Have Leonardo come and see me," commanded Don Julio.

"I am afraid that won't be possible because Arnulfo took Leonardo with him," answered the man with a shaky voice.

"You sent him away too? Are you out of your mind! You'd better go and bring him back immediately!"

"I did not authorize Arnulfo to take him. You know I had him working at the market place, just like you requested. Arnulfo took him without asking me! You should know that he sometimes hides things from you and me!"

Fermín started towards the door and then Don Julio called him back.

"Wait! Maybe that is not such a bad idea. No questions asked during the Jaripeo. Tell me exactly when will they return?"

"On Thursday morning sir," said Fermín.

"Go to the arena. We are already late," ordered Don Julio in a calmer voice.

Fermín went out fuming. On one thing he did agree with the boss; that would be the last time he needed his consent for anything. He went through the kitchen, took a sip of fresh water, and slammed the clay mug on the floor. Beatriz, Estela, and Santiago were back from the stables already. They were getting dressed for the occasion.

JARIPEO

The sun was beginning to throw a lean shadow on the west bleachers of the arena. The whole multitude awaited the arrival of the Cieneguilla Estate showcase ride. The Cortez Family led the team on fine colts. Don Julio's hand-worked saddle was mainly made with bone and silver. It contrasted his horse's bright blackness. Mrs. Cortez waved standing on a horse carriage. She was dressed in elegant French apparel. Next to her was a prancing white, Andalucian, Arabian steed. The black lace that adorned Beatriz' beige dress, emphasized her beauty and lifted her confidence. As soon as they entered the circle, the crowd exploded in cheers welcoming the hosts and the beginning of the festivities. The Cortez Family roamed around waving and welcoming their main guests. Beatriz impressed everyone with her ability to ride and to command the beast. Santiago was truly impressed by such a beautiful woman. Don Julio called the crowd's attention and acknowledged the Regidor's presence. He also welcomed the other Hacendados and wished them luck in the competition. After presenting all the judges, he then turned to the local priest and had him give a short sermon on gratitude. Right after the priest had blessed the event, the multitude was startled by the fireworks right above their heads. It was indeed the official start of the village carnival.

The marching band played blissful tunes during the contest. It was evident that Guanajuato, Santiago's team, was superior. They won most of the competition except horse breaking and blind folded riding. The Regidor's son boasted explaining why they had won. Eleodoro was annoyed just to see him. Don Julio was disappointed to see his team lose at every event. He still held a heavy heart against Fermín but pretended to be enjoying the show. He almost rooted for every second place, but his pride stamped out his voice. Beatriz was eager to go back home and rest for a while. She realized that Eleodoro was waiting for her answer, and it was hard to break his heart. She tried to convince herself why it wasn't possible to court him, but there still existed strong possibilities.

"The Fuentes Family might have sufficient economic resources to solve my family's financial troubles. Then, my best friend Estela can be part of my family, and I don't have to live far away from my mother! That's not bad at all. But then attending school in Europe with Eleodoro might also work. It is such a difficult decision now that Santiago is becoming a good friend!" she thought.

The show finally ended. Hosts and guests returned to the main quarters for the afternoon. After dinner, an informal social gathering took place in the ballroom. Santiago wanted to spend the afternoon with Beatriz, but Eleodoro's comments caught his attention one more time.

"As you see, my house El Tequesquite Hacienda, has taken two competitions for the day. It is proof that we are becoming better," he alleged, looking directly at Santiago, "sooner or later we will surpass the team ahead."

"We deserve a little bit of credit for taking horse breaking and the blindfold riding, but what really matters is the race," his father explained trying to soften the comment.

"Why don't we have an elimination race tomorrow and the final on Friday?" suggested Santiago challenging everyone, "That will shut some mouths and allow the elite racers, deservingly, to compete for the cup a second time."

"Do you mean the four or five that come first will do it again on Friday?" asked one of the Hacendados.

"Let's do the first six, so every estate runs with the best horse they have," explained the bachelor.

"It seems that everyone likes the idea. Are you willing to do that?" called Don Julio out loud after consulting with the Regidor.

Everyone accepted the plan enthusiastically. They figured the race was one of the main reasons to hold the Jaripeo. Don Julio sent word to the stables. Everyone needed to get ready for the race the following afternoon. Eleodoro gave a note to his sister Estela to deliver to Beatriz. He wanted to see her that night in the garden by the water fountain. Beatriz was hesitant to attend but was troubled to leave him without an answer.

"Can you please tell your brother to wait? I need more than a week to think about it. Tell him that I will have an answer when everyone leaves," explained Beatriz.

That night Cirilo del Castillo and his son had a private conversation. Santiago wanted to hear his father's opinion about Beatriz and her family.

"But you don't want to formalize a relationship with this young lady yet, is that correct?" questioned the Regidor, "it would be too soon."

"What if we extend a formal invitation for the Cortez Family to come to Guanajuato for a few weeks? That way, I can have more time to court her and study her manners," recommended Santiago.

"Two weeks are more than sufficient time. Don Julio has business to attend, and I don't think he would be willing. He was just there last week," said the Regidor.

"He would not say no to the Regidor. I'm sincerely fond of this woman. I would like to spend more time with her. What do you think about her?"

"You have good taste. She has her own mind, but she can be taught," replied the father.

"That's why I need time with her. What about the family? Are they good enough for us?"

Santiago asked with hope in his heart.

"I am still hoping for someone in Europe. We have an agreement! Don't forget our class! Royalty runs in our veins. The Duke from Leon is a better match. His daughter is madly in love with you," reminded the Regidor.

"Yes, I have not forgotten. But Beatriz would be a great replacement," replied Santiago.

Unexpectedly, Don Julio joined them, so they changed the conversation. There was a strange conspiracy going on between father and son, and it now included Beatriz. Cirilo's distant relative in Leon, Spain, had a typhus dying daughter. There was a marriage arrangement between the families. With such a marriage, Santiago will receive a title from the Crown. The Duke's family will see their daughter happy for the rest of her short life. There was a legal document already which disclaimed any wealth to the Castillo Family. Santiago wanted his father to arrange a locking marriage agreement with Beatriz the following year.

The next morning breakfast was a repetition of the day before. Santiago and Eleodoro were trying to impress Beatriz and arrogantly predicted the race outcome. Don Julio and Cirilo conversed about business, politics, and common European acquaintances.

Word was out. The preliminary race would take place at El Camino Real at one o'clock. The five Hacendados and the Regidor would need time to check with their horse tenders and racers.

At the stables, Miguel had his three stallions brushed and shined again. He was confident about this year's competition. Fifteen colts were registered to run. Three belonged to Don Julio, and three belonged to Cirilo. A black stallion mounted by Santiago was the favorite to win the race. The racing track was really the main road and then deviated towards the lagoon, covering a total of eight kilometers. The finish line was just on the crossways. A sufficient crowd had already gathered. They stood adjacent to the track. Beatriz and Estela secured a place on the temporary stands near the road. They sat just behind their parents. Don Julio was worried about finishing last. That meant harassment for a whole year.

On the start line, Santiago wore a red bandana on his head and tried to pacify his stallion. Eleodoro was by him riding a walnut steed. He was wearing a white bandana on his head. Both men looked at each other ignoring the other racers completely. It was more than a race. It meant an evening with Beatriz and a chance to impress her. At the far left, Miguel was ready for full gallop. He wore a black bandana on his head.

The gun was fired. The horses dashed leaving a cloud of dust. It was hard to see who was in the lead. Cirilo and Don Julio shared a lens to find out their position in the race. Racers passed the storage house at full speed. A brown stallion appeared clearly at the front. It was Miguel. He was two full bodies ahead of Eleodoro who cut in front of Santiago. It was only the beginning. Positions for sure would change on the way back. It was announced that Don Julio's rider was in the lead. He felt an impulse to boast but controlled his emotions. Beatriz was anxious to see them back already. There was a whole commotion of hopes and expectations in the crowd. By this time, the racers had reached the open field on their way to the lagoon. They needed to come around the field and back into the main road. It was announced that Miguel had lost the lead and now followed in second place. Eleodoro was catching up to him, but Santiago was hard to identify.

"I see him! I see him!" shouted the Regidor, "he is coming strong all the way to the front."

Beatriz asked to borrow the lens but was not interested in finding Santiago. She was disappointed to see Miguel trailing at the end. She looked for the other black bandanas. They were not in the front either.

"How are we doing?" asked Don Julio.

"Not too well," answered the girl.

Don Julio took the lens and confirmed the bad news. He was able to see the black bandana riders in last place. He quickly put the lens down and handed it to Cirilo who extended his hand.

"Eleodoro is first! We are winning the race!" exclaimed Ramon, his father, standing on the bleachers.

The racers were on their way back now approaching the storage rooms. They prepared to execute the final five hundred meters. The lens was not needed anymore. It was evident that Eleodoro, wearing a white bandana, was in first place. As he past the buildings, a loud breathing caught his attention. It was Santiago whipping his beast to the finish line. His black colt was still full of stamina and easily emerged ahead of the rest. The crowd exploded when the racers crossed the finish line. It was a great come back for Santiago who crossed the finish line first. He was followed by another Guanajuato rider. In third place, Eleodoro struggled to beat another rider. It was a total disappointment to see the host team come in last place.

Don Julio was in total silence as the Regidor celebrated his victory. Santiago, who was on foot now, came back quickly to honor Beatriz and dedicate his triumph to her.

"We should do it again on Friday," said the Regidor. "Come on! Change your face. You have another chance in two days!"

"Against such competition? Save me the embarrassment. I don't think I'll even compete," said Don Julio as he shook Santiago's hand.

"Now, may I have permission to dance with your daughter on Friday evening?" asked Santiago arrogantly.

"You certainly deserve it. Of course you can," responded the Hacendado.

Beatriz smiled and acted as if she had cheered for him all the way. She just knew what the topic would be for the rest of the day. Eleodoro came by them and continued to press forward on his quest.

"You said you would dance with the loser. That's why I didn't win."

"And that would be Miguel, wouldn't it?" answered the girl in a serious tone.

"It was only between Santiago and me," he claimed.

Santiago pushed him aside and opened way for the girl. They continued all the way home followed by the rest of the guests. Don Julio called an emergency meeting with his stewards. He walked all the way to the storage building to blow off his steam.

"It was such a lousy performance! Last place in the race is inconceivable! Were you aware of our horses' horrendous speed?" questioned the boss.

Fermín and the administrator blamed Arnulfo and his people for the poor performance.

"I will not be embarrassed again! From this moment on, we will pull out of any competition," Don Julio dictated.

He ordered them to serve the Regidor's team carefully in their needs. He also demanded a full report on sales and merchandise.

"Have ready the special load I asked you to prepare by Saturday morning," he said, "It is my gift for such a distinguished visit from Guanajuato. I also need to know when the horses get here!"

He shortly returned to the main quarters because he wanted to be near the Regidor. Once in the house, the Regidor wanted to speak to him privately.

"I have enjoyed this time away from the city. I am grateful for all your attention and how things have worked out. Besides winning the race and getting to know you, it is about my son Santiago that I need to say a few words."

"He is charmed with your daughter; however, he is also considering Ramon's daughter. He is seriously contemplating a formal courtship after he makes a final decision. I fully support his wish, but I need to request your permission if he chooses your daughter. Do you oppose that?"

It was music to Don Julio's ears. His face was full of emotion. His terrible day turned around into a bright, hopeful reality.

"Beatriz is my only descendant. You see; my hopes are placed on her decisions. I don't see a better match for her than Santiago," responded Don Julio. "They have my full support to get to know each other. Your son needs to be careful…Beatriz and Estela are very close friends."

Santiago and Beatriz took a ride to the vineyards that afternoon. They were driven in a carriage that had to wait on the main road. They walked to the creek and then in to the rows. It was a chance for Beatriz to get to know him better.

"What do you see in me?" she asked.

"I see a bright, beautiful woman who needs to know what true love is," he answered, puzzled by her question.

"What makes you think I don't know what true love is?"

"You don't know what true love is because you don't know me. If you consent to it, I can become your true love," Santiago bragged.

"It is too soon to know because true love must be felt by both hearts and that takes time.

True love is not something you find; it is something you create. Couples get married when they attain such a feeling, but they must continue to nourish and cherish such sentiment," Beatriz explained.

Santiago was cornered with her answer. At first he thought she was proposing to him, he later realized that he didn't exist in her heart.

"Don't get me wrong. When I bring up marriage, I don't do it to hint anything. I look at marriage as the most important event in a person's life."

"I think of it the same way," he said taking her hand, "Do I have a chance to become your true love?"

Beatriz was tense. Her parent's wish came to her mind, and now it all depended on her answer.

"Since nothing discourages you, I would say you might. Let's walk around this row and pick some grapes," Beatriz suggested leading ahead and changing the subject.

They filled the basket in silence but looked at each other. Santiago had made up his mind.

"I will not rest until this woman falls at my feet."

The next day, a full battalion showed up around the property. It was intended to deter any rebellion among the farmers. The squad entered the arena right before the ring race. Beatriz and Estella sat in the front row. The ring race was held in their honor. A gold ring hanging from a string in the middle of the arena would be presented to one of the girls by the winner. Santiago and Eleodoro refused to lose this competition. Armed with a short wooden lance, opponents took turns racing in full gallop, attempting to skewer the ring with their lance. Just like Eleodoro predicted, his estate was becoming better. With a sharp eye and split-second timing, he took the ring. It was an atrocious blow to Santiago's pride. The bachelor swallowed his anger when Eleodoro presented the ring to Beatriz.

"Please don't erase my name from this competition. This ring is a symbol of my affection for you!" Ramon's son exclaimed.

"Felicidades! You were outstanding!" Beatriz corresponded.

Transactions continued at the market. Most provisions were almost sold out. Loaded carts with goods of all sorts packed the main road as they left Don Julio's quarters. A tour of the orchards and vineyards was scheduled for the afternoon. The Regidor was interested in finding out the Hacienda's potential to gain interest. He needed to estimate taxes and find out how much Don Julio really owned. Inadvertently, he was really checking the five Hacendados' capital and assets. Arnulfo and Leonardo were expected to return today, but there was no sign of them. Don Julio was becoming impatient. He had already sent his men to find them.

Far away in the Alamito Valley, Arnulfo and Leonardo were busy leading a heard of wild mesteños on their way back to the Hacienda. They galloped back and forth, yelling and whistling, dodging in and out through clouds of spinning dust, cracking whips, and waving sombreros. Two rough days and a night with little sleep finally slowed down their expedition. Leonardo's eyes were reddish and totally disobeyed his will to stay open. Arnulfo's cowboys refused to go any longer. They would rather camp and round up the horses the next day.

"Bear with me one more hour! You can do it! We will get the stallions into the canyon and close both ends," the vet explained, "We will then split up and camp on both sides."

The canyon served as a corral; nonetheless, it was not the safest shelter against thieves. Arnulfo's biggest fear was being intercepted by rebel forces.

"The Realist army will protect us when they learn this herd is for the Regidor's soldiers, but what will you tell insurgents if they halt us?" Leonardo inquired.

"Don't say that out loud! My worst fear is to be accused of supplying horses to government soldiers. I hope we don't see either group," Arnulfo whispered rebuking the tired young man.

The band of cowboys reluctantly pushed all they way to the canyon. It was almost dinner time when they saw the lower eroded creeks disappear into the canyon.

"Hold your horses, cowboys!" shouted Arnulfo after a whistle, "Let's stop here!"

Stopping was a challenge because the herd continued moving forward into all directions.

"Half of us will camp on this side of the canyon. The other seven will do it on the other side. You have to go away and around the herd to enter the ravine. You must do so without directing the mustangs from the trail. Is that clear?" the horse whisperer explained.

"Go with them Leonardo! Make sure you block the north side completely."

Leonardo was hoping to stay. He was afraid of falling asleep and falling down. The other six riders knew exactly what to do because they had been in previous round ups. They quickly detoured far to the right and forward. The remaining cowboys dismounted and walked around to stretch their legs. They would wait for the gun shot and then lead the wild horses into the canyon. Arnulfo directed two other men to go far to the left, just in case the herd ran in that direction.

After a while, Leonardo and company entered the canyon. He was straggling behind and thought he saw someone spying on them.

"It must be my imagination. No one seems to stop or say anything!" he thought.

"I wonder if Beatriz misses me. I was looking forward to see her ride in the parade, and now I missed it! She probably looked stunning on Lightning's back! I can't wait to see her!"

Arnulfo and the rest of the group were ready to camp after securing all the horses down into the canyon. His men moved some rocks and dry branches attempting to block the entrance. They also built a fire right on the trail.

"Do I have a volunteer to be the watchman while the rest of us take a nap?"

Nobody answered. He had no choice than to volunteer himself.

"Go ahead. I will stay up. We will take turns every two hours."

The horses had no way out and grazed in the middle of the narrow valley. The cowboys quickly fell sound asleep including the watchman. They had no idea what an easy target they became for the band of thieves who secretly spied on them. The bandits advanced nimbly towards Leonardo's camp.

"Seize their weapons before we wake them up!" the intruder whispered walking in Leonardo's direction.

"Get up sleepy dog! Don't do anything foolish, or I'll fill your head with lead!"

Leonardo thought it was a nightmare, yet the kick on his shoulder was real. The musket's barrel on his nose scared away his fatigue.

"Where are you going? Who is the person in charge?" demanded the intruder.

The cowboys remained silent. Their fear froze their tongue, and no one muttered a word.

"We are on an errand! We belong to the Cieneguilla Hacienda! Don Julio Cortez is our boss," replied Leonardo, being the bravest among them.

"He was your boss! You have a new one starting right now! ME! You're no longer cowboys. You are now soldiers in the people's revolution!"

At that moment, gun fire from all directions encompassed the camp. The thieves fled through the creeks when they noticed Realist soldiers approaching from the north. It was General Calleja and the best assembled army on their way to Guadalajara. After the gunfire, the army only found dead bodies and two dead horses at the canyon exit. After the soldiers verified that no one was alive, they secured the area

"Did you identify any of them?" the General demanded.

"It seems that thieves were buying cavalry from some cowboys, but they are all dead now! There is a wild herd down in the ravine," the major replied.

"That will be our payment! Secure as many as possible!"

The Realist officer was pleased to see the wild horses and took twenty horses as a reward. They continued on their way, deviating west and avoiding the canyon. At the other side of the canyon, Arnulfo and his men remained unaffected and slept like a log.

Back at the Hacienda, a secret conversation was taking place in one of the storage rooms. It was Fermín and five other men.

"On Friday, the market will be closed for the main race. At six a clock, everyone should be eating and talking about the events of the day. The two of you will start the fire in this room. As soon as everyone rushes to put it out, you will burn all the hay at the stables too. Remember! Wait until you hear the gun fire. That will be your sign. Now, Martin, you have the most important assignment of the night. You will be serving in the ball room. I will give you the platter with the drinks. Don't mistake them. I will put three spoons next to the glasses and the bottle. Ramon, Don Julio, and the Regidor will surely be together. They will close with a toast."

Fermín had carefully designed his evil plan. It included a secret message to rebel forces. They would come to reinforce his ambition. He had promised a safe haven for revolutionaries if he were aided.

"What about the soldiers? Will they be gone by tomorrow?" asked one of the men.

"Don't worry about them. The lieutenant and I have an agreement. He is one of us," assured Fermín. "A new order has begun, and it is our turn to rule!" boasted Fermín. "By now, my contacts have seized the blacksmith shop in Teocaltiche."

The next day was full of anticipation. Men had returned without finding a trace of Arnulfo and his men. It was assumed that rebel forces had intercepted them and taken them captive. Don Julio was worried because the army was already on his property and he had no way to pay them. The troop was parading along the main road, making line formations and showcasing weapons.

That evening, a great commotion caused panic among the guests. Word came to Don Julio that something terrible happened to Arnulfo. He was brought home lying in the back of a cart. The vet was taken through the settlements, across the stables, all the way to his house. When Don Julio and Fermín came to his house, they were terrified to see his hand swollen and disfigured. It was accented by an intense bluish, black color from his finger tips to his arm. The mark of two rattle snake fangs on the back of Arnulfo's hand stood out. He was dying. The only way to save him was to amputate the arm. A heavy trunk chop was brought. His screams were heard all the way to the storage room. Now, it was only a matter of time. Three out of five survived a rattle snake bite. Another rider from the Hacienda was also bitten, but he perished on the road.

The Jaripeo had to go on. Don Julio was appeased to know that the rest of his men would arrive with the herd anytime. It was also reported that only thirty beasts were on their way and that revolutionaries took most of the cavalry. Now Don Julio would need to compensate the army with silver coins and only thirty horses. The violent gun fire at the canyon had taken the lives of half the company. No word of Leonardo's fate.

It was almost midnight, but the cowboys never came. Don Julio had assigned Fermín to watch the whole night. He wanted to see the herd in the corral the next morning. Fermín went and came along the main road. He rode all the way to the south side of the Hacienda several times.

Mourn

It was five in the morning at the Hacienda. A tall, grouchy looking figure was active on the main quarter's porch. It was Fermín. His raccoon looking eyes revealed a sleepless night. He was waiting to tell the boss about the anticipated errand. His body surrendered to fatigue, and he finally fell asleep on a bench just outside the door. Two hours later, he was awakened by the sunlight and the people's noise. He was dismissed as soon as he spoke to Don Julio.

The kitchen table was as busy as it had been the whole week. Martina looked for an opportunity to talk to Beatriz about the vet's daughter. She hesitated because it wasn't what Beatriz wanted to hear. Before Don Julio's daughter sat down for breakfast, the maid gestured to her to come into the kitchen.

"I interrogated Elena two days ago. She accused you and your father of taking advantage of Leonardo. She said that you had stolen his horse," the maid explained.

"Did she say anything about Leonardo's feelings towards her?"

"She pretended to be involved with him since long ago. She even hopes Leonardo will marry her. I know she cooked for him and mended his face one time when Fermín hurt him," Martina explained.

"I don't need to hear anymore. This helps me make a better decision," Beatriz replied before she returned to the table.

The conversation at the table was all about Arnulfo and his men. Don Julio shared about the violent trip, totally confirming the Regidor's warnings.

"Five of my men were killed by thieves on the way back from the Alamito Valley. I can affirm it was infidel thieves because they knew when to strike. They took most of the horses."

"Do we know who perished on the errand?" asked Mrs. Cortez.

"Yes, they were two of Arnulfo's men; one was killed by a rattle snake. Another two were recruited by Fermín from the orchards. The last one was Leonardo Valle. I had hired him recently to help in the stables," Don Julio explained.

Beatriz dropped her glass when she heard the news. A feeling of grief and guilt suffocated her chest. She sat quietly as Santiago padded the spilled water with his cloth.

"Are they confirmed casualties or prisoners? Sometimes the rebels convince their prisoners to join their forces," said the Regidor.

Beatriz hoped for that. She realized that Leonardo would have taken any chance to join the fight for equality. She also discovered her true feelings for Leonardo. Her tears revealed the emptiness in her heart. She asked to be excused from the table and left directly for her chamber. She was followed by her mother who sensed her daughter's feelings.

The Jaripeo's main event was scheduled at noon. Every estate would be represented except Don Julio's. He refused to be embarrassed again. Ramon, from El Tequesquite, had already given him a hard time. His son Eleodoro was ready for a rematch.

Shortly after, only Ramon and Don Julio remained at the table. It was then that Don Julio realized how clever Cirilo Del Castillo played his game.

"The Regidor has invited me to spend a week at his mansion. I will be there next month," said Ramon, "his son is very interested in my daughter Estela. Our families will use that time to get to know each other better. I share this with you because I know that your daughter might have had her hopes up."

"When did he invite you?" asked Don Julio.

"Just last night when you were at the stables," replied Ramon.

"But I don't see Santiago following your daughter as much as he follows mine. We need to be careful that he doesn't hurt their feelings."

"He might spend more time with Beatriz because she's hosting him. That will change once they leave your home." Ramon explained, looking at his best friend.

"Do you know if he has invited anybody else besides you?" Don Julio asked.

"I don't think so. Only you and I have a daughter. Has he invited you?" asked the man.

"Yes. I will be there in two weeks. He has also accepted an invitation to spend Christmas here," commented Don Julio, trying to hide his lie.

"Come on Julio! He is not going to divide our friendship, is he?" inquired the visiting Hacendado.

Before Don Julio replied, the Regidor walked in. Both men remained silent for a moment and then got up to acknowledge their superior. It was the perfect time to confront him, but both men were afraid to be left aside.

"Do you want me to lend you one of my race stallions so you can join the competition?" taunted the Regidor, followed by a laugh.

"You are guaranteed at least sixth place," Ramon said joining the Regidor laughing.

"You have to fire your horse tender. I can even lend you one if you want!" mocked Cirilo.

"Maybe the rattle snake incident is just a trick by your top cowboy to avoid a beating!" Ramon added in a sarcastic laugh.

"No. He is really sick. His arm had to be amputated last night," Don Julio explained defensively.

"That harsh are your beatings that he'd rather lose an arm than be blamed for losing the race?" the Regidor teased.

Don Julio was irritated by their comment and lack of empathy. He excused himself and went to his bedroom to get ready for the main event. It was definite; his estate would not be represented in the race. He summoned Beatriz to his room. After a moment, she came in accompanied by his wife.

"So how are things working out between you and Santiago?"

"Don't worry I have fulfilled my part of the agreement. We are good friends now," she replied.

"Today, you left him alone at the table! What happened?" he demanded.

"It was the news about the young man, the one you brought to help her with the horse, Leonardo," his wife explained, "she had also become friends with him."

"Are you sure he died?" Beatriz asked as she wiped her tears.

"Fermín confirmed only the ones who made it back. He wasn't one of them," clarified the boss, "but you should change your attitude. It wasn't Santiago who perished. Tell me that you would feel the same way for Santiago."

"Father, you are pressuring me. You can't force me to love someone I just met!" Beatriz protested with a sob.

"I don't understand you! Are you crying for Leonardo? He is a servant who you just also met!" Don Julio questioned. "Tell me that you didn't place your eyes on an Indian. You know I would die of disappointment!"

"It doesn't matter! He isn't here anymore! He is dead!" cried the young woman, seeking to embrace her mother to ease her grief.

"You need to lower your voices! Someone will hear you!" Beatriz' mother whispered.

"You need to get over it! Go and clean your face. We need to be at the race in an hour!" he commanded.

Don Julio motioned for his wife to take Beatriz out of the room. He just sat on the bed analyzing his daughter's comments and expression. He felt he was also losing the race to the Regidor's fortune. It was time to get a real commitment from the Regidor, or to accept Ramon's son's offer as a consolation. He was aware of Eleodoro's intentions towards Beatriz.

Everyone was anxiously waiting at the main entrance. Santiago was the favorite again. He was also pounding Eleodoro with his comments.

"Europe will always be sort of a paternal mentor to the new world. It is evidenced by the very sounds that come out of your mouth. The Castilian language is a gift you will never hide. The respect and patriotism for the crown and the church will be written in your history, and most of all, the literature and the arts will always run in your veins."

"As you can see, some people may migrate to the moon, and they may establish the same traditions without denting the status quo! Not here in America! This land is a land of awakening, a land where people are not afraid to reform that which has failed. Truly a land of promise! We will retain the best from Europe but establish new frontiers," lectured Eleodoro.

"Let me have everyone's attention! Besides showing who the number one rider is, we should find out who the better man is. Don Julio and Beatriz have agreed to honor the winner at the ball tonight. Let's put it this way. The winner will sit by Beatriz and dance to every piece of music with her," Santiago announced just when Don Julio showed up, "I will prove it again. I am the better man! There is really no competition at all!"

Everyone cheered because they saw no better racer to take the trophy. They also liked the couple Beatriz and Santiago. Don Julio loved the idea but feared that someone might upset them. He came to Santiago to wish him good luck.

"I need to have a word with you in private," Don Julio said taking Santiago to the side, "I see that you and Beatriz are getting along fine. Why do you want to dance with her tonight?"

Before he could answer Cirilo Del Castillo joined them.

"Your daughter is a lovely woman. I am charmed by her gentle ways and her brightness. I like her very much," the bachelor replied.

"She is not a trophy. Do you understand what I mean?" asked the Hacendado.

"Yes, I do. I will never play with her feelings."

"Julio, you have to trust him. If my son wins, allow him to spend the evening with Beatriz. It can be in our presence or the garden. If he loses, accept an invitation to my house for a week. That way, Beatriz can really get to know Santiago," the Regidor proposed.

"Do you mean that if your son loses the race, my family gets to spend a week in your house? You are a clever man. You know you have a greater possibility of winning. Is that why you offer?" protested Don Julio, "Did you make the same offer to Ramon?"

"Not at all, my son is interested in your daughter, not his. Isn't that right Santiago?"

"That is true," Santiago confirmed.

"I did agree that if Ramon's son wins the race, his family may come to Guanajuato for a week. You have to understand that he is competing against me, and you have chickened out," Cirilo explained with a smile.

They shook hands and began walking towards the main road which now was the race track. Santiago went ahead because he needed to go all the way to the stables.

Beatriz and her mother also came out of the house on their way to the stands. They were followed by their maids who held umbrellas to provide shade. On the street, the guards were ushering people out to the race track. The finish line was right in front of the highest seats on the road. It was the Regidor and the Hacendado's families who packed that bleacher. The tumultuous crowd chanted Santiago's name. They had seen his horse, and he had conquered their hearts. No one remembered Eleodoro at all.

It was ten minutes before the main event. Don Julio had second thoughts. He was perturbed by the idea of Eleodoro winning the race. He loved that idea, but it also meant that Ramon and Estela would have the same chance. He realized how cunning the Regidor was and how he needed to come up with something to surprise him.

The Race

In the distance, there was a man running in the middle of the race track. The guards did not stop him because he had a racer's bandana on his head. It was Miguel, the vet's son. As soon as the crowd noticed which team he belonged to, they began booing. He had a message for Don Julio, but the boss was embarrassed to see him.

"What are you doing here? I told you we were out of the race!" the Hacendado questioned.

"Señor, I have a message from Fermín. It is also a message from the people at the stables. We want to run this race. We need your approval. Please! It is my father's wish!" the cowboy begged.

"Come on Julio, join in! You are already in last place. How worse can it be? This is your chance to redeem yourself!" Ramon pressured.

"That's right. You wouldn't lose anything!" the Regidor encouraged.

Don Julio looked at them and then turned to his wife. She nodded in the affirmative.

"As long as it is somebody besides you racing, you have my permission," Don Julio blurted, feeling that his men were challenging his decision.

"I am your best rider!" the young man mumbled, rushing back to the stables.

The rider took off, waving the bandana on his hand. He was only two minutes away from the main event. Beatriz was sitting at the top row accompanied by Estela, Martina, and other young people. They were the most energetic in the crowd. She was surrounded by her friends and most likely the future ruling generation, but she felt alone. On the other side of the road, she saw a familiar face. She was intrigued that the woman was cheerful. It was Elena and the people from the stables.

"How can she forget him so quickly," Beatriz thought, "she never loved him. I was his only true love."

She was awakened by a gun shot which announced the beginning of the competition. When she turned to look; the cloud of dust impeded her view of the horses. She wasn't aware that her father's estate was competing. The Regidor had the lens to himself because Don Julio refused to use it when it was offered to him. From the roof of the Hacienda, a man with a telescope held up the leading color. Eleodoro was in the front. Racers were just past the storage house. They still needed to continue all the way to the lagoon and back. Don Julio and Ramon hoped that Eleodoro would stay in the front until the end. The Regidor totally trusted his son Santiago. He was the most experienced rider. He had years of training at the best race tracks in Europe. The bachelor also had the best horses in New Spain. It was a race; both Eleodoro and Santiago led the herd. It was not clear who was ahead, but both were by the lagoon now.

A rested Fermín joined his boss. Don Julio walked down two steps towards him and demanded an explanation.

"What is going on at the stables? Why are you making these kinds of decisions? We better not finish last!"

"I beg your pardon! I haven't been to the stables since dawn today. What decisions?" Fermín replied.

"Miguel just came and told me you decided to put a racer on the track! If you didn't order it, who did it then?" Don Julio shouted.

Fermín denied knowing anything about it, despite the fact that he approved it. He knew they didn't have a chance to win, but it was a part of his plan to embarrass the boss. Losing again would benefit his plan.

The crowd's noise interrupted the chastisement because the man on the roof announced the racer ahead. The riders were all the way to the lagoon now and on the way back to the finish line. This was the race everyone anticipated. It was the one event to remember and talk about the whole year.

"Yes! They are on their way back just before the storage rooms. I am ahead!" cried the Regidor handing the lens to Ramon, "it is only between you and me, Ramon!"

"No! Eleodoro is ahead now and it is only him and I ahead!" Ramon shouted signaling to the man in the roof to change the color.

The man on the roof kept changing colors. He put up red and then white as if he were waving both colors. As the racers went behind the storage rooms, an unknown rider on a potent stallion surfaced from behind. He was in a mad dash easily emerging in the front. The crowd, unaware, chanted for Santiago and Eleodoro only to be silenced by a true lightning on the track.

"There is a new leader!" shouted the crowd.

"Who is that?" inquired a perplexed Regidor putting the lens down since it wasn't necessary anymore.

"IT IS CIENEGUILLA! IT IS CIENEGUILLA!" people screamed.

"But who is that rider with the black bandana?" asked Don Julio with incredulous eyes. Across the street, people began to say his name. All the commotion caught Beatriz's attention. When she recognized the rider, her heart jumped out of rhythm. The leading man appeared imposing, just like a knight in shining armor, riding a heavenly white horse.

"LEONARDO! It is Leonardo!" she screamed, running down the steps just when he crossed the finish line.

"WE WON! WE WON!" a jubilant Don Julio jumped, hugging his wife and hitting Fermín on the head.

He felt on top of the world again. He turned to an astonished Regidor and smiled with a victorious look.

"Never count me out! I always have a come back," Don Julio told Ramon.

"But where did you find such a rider? I am impressed!" the Regidor said.

All the Hacendados came to congratulate Don Julio personally. They felt the victory was also theirs since it was the first time the city's team was defeated. It sure would go down in the history of Hacendados. As they digested such an upset, the crowd carried Leonardo on their shoulders. He had been a prisoner for a few hours and then let go by rebel forces. He came at dawn, and no one knew of his existence until half an hour before the race. The Vallejo kid was now a hero to the entire Hacienda. Fermín's plan to embarrass the boss and to brand Leonardo as insubordinate had failed.

Among hundreds of euphoric people, a sobbing woman found her way. Her tearful black eyes only saw one person. From a distance, Leonardo recognized her.

"Beatriz! Beatriz! Put me down! Put me down!" demanded the young man who then forged his way through the people.

Right in the middle of the road, exactly under the finish line they met in an embrace. It was the very same magical tenderness they felt the first time they met. Such a feeling cleared Beatriz's confusion and filled her empty heart. Leonardo longed to feel her heartbeat and breathe her gentle hair's scent.

Outside the circular love aura, Santiago, Eleodoro, and Elena endured a bitter defeat. They couldn't believe what they saw. From the stands, the Regidor immediately recognized the winner, but before he said a word, Ramon called out,

"You made a promise and you must keep your word!" he said looking at Don Julio and Cirilo, "That young man deserves to be recognized at the ball tonight. He should have the first dance with our daughters if he wishes!"

"Oh yes, sure. He is one of my leaders at the stable!" announced Don Julio.

"I would attest that I have seen him before! What's his name?" asked the Regidor.

"I need to talk to you at another time," requested Don Julio feeling a sigh stuck in his throat.

In the middle of the road, a jealous Santiago, who got second place only defeating the third rider by a nose, approached Beatriz.

"And this is?" Santiago said looking at Beatriz.

"This is…" hesitated Beatriz.

"Leonardo, Leonardo Vallejo," responded the cowboy extending a handshake.

"He is my trainer. He helped me get ready for the Jaripeo," the woman explained.

"Weren't you dead? You came from your tomb to spoil my victory!" cried Santiago in an arrogant tone and ignoring his hand.

"It has been agreed and announced that you will be Señorita Beatriz's partner this evening," interrupted Eleodoro, pointing to Leonardo and trying to rub in a local victory, "and you Santiago, as the first runner up, will pay tribute and present him the laurel emblem at the ball."

"Can I see you before dinner? We need to talk!" Leonardo asked turning to Beatriz and ignoring the racers.

"We need to talk to my father right away," the girl replied.

"Well done, Leonardo. I am relieved to see you are all right!" Don Julio called as he and the others joined them.

"Don Julio, I am glad to see you again! I need to tell you that…"

"Not now! You will join us for dinner. You can tell me anything you want there. Go on and change. Meet us at the ballroom," Don Julio interrupted.

"Santiago my friend, my family and I will stay with your family for a week. You will spend enough time with Beatriz. Your father has been so kind to extend such an invitation," Don Julio continued turning to Cirilo del Castillo.

"I have always kept my promises and so does my son. Tonight, Santiago will allow that young man to be honored as he deserves. And you Julio, he saved your neck! What a great come back!" the Regidor admitted.

The crowd seized Leonardo again and took him all the way to the stables. Before that, he made sure his Arabian horse was taken by Miguel. Once in Arnulfo's house, he first came to see the vet. Arnulfo was boiling in a fever. It was a good sign that he would live. There was such a contrast in mood among the family. Only Miguel and Elena left the house to attend the stables. It was a great relief to know that Arnulfo's team won the race. They had pleased their boss more than any servant in the estate.

Last Dance

Back at the main quarters, Beatriz had a second plan in case her father disagreed. She was packing a leather bag. It gave the impression that she was preparing to go on a far away trip. She had also written a goodbye letter to her mother letting her know she would be leaving with Leonardo. She was about to write the name of the place but a knock on her door interrupted her. It was Mrs. Cortez. She wanted to know if she was ready but left after a negative response. Beatriz threw the letter inside the bag with the intent to finish it later. For that evening, she found a dark blue gown to impress all the aristocracy. She kept on looking out her window, hoping Leonardo would be there. Don Julio and the Regidor were at the library behind locked doors.

"Leonardo, the young man who won the race is Joaquin's son!" Don Julio whispered.

"Good grief! You are full of surprises. What is he doing here in your Hacienda?" Cirilo asked.

"He is an orphan. I've taken him under my wing. He is being prepared to go to Spain. He will study medicine."

"That's nice of you," the Regidor said, "How does he know your daughter so well?"

"They both have been taking classes from Carmelo de la Cruz, the professor I hired to prepare my daughter for the University. Leonardo also accompanied her when she practiced her mounting skills. But I need your silence. Joaquin had bitter enemies. I took a big risk by bringing Leonardo here. What if they want revenge? No one knows he is here." Don Julio explained.

"My friend, don't worry about me. I purchased La Casa Grande from Antonio. It was a real bargain, I couldn't resist. Antonio will join us in Guanajuato when you come. We will finish the transaction then."

Don Julio was speechless to hear that. He truly was amazed by the Regidor's cleverness. He thought he was so ahead of him.

"The Casa Grande! Joaquin Vallejo's estate is yours now?" Don Julio inquired.

"That's right. It will become Santiago's trust once he learns the ups and downs in New Spain," explained the Regidor, "that's why I needed to know if Joaquin had any survivors."

"Are you going to present Leonardo with his father's medal?" Don Julio asked.

"No. I said that just to get more information about La Casa Grande and my transaction," Cirlio replied.

"Why don't we merge our friendship and families into something more formal?" Don Julio suggested.

"What do you mean?"

"Yes. Santiago likes my daughter and my daughter loves Santiago. How about marriage between the two?" proposed Don Julio feeling his stomach and heart losing stability.

"To be honest with you, I really like that idea! As Santiagos's father in law, you can look out for him when I am away in Guanajuato. He is fascinated by your daughter but there is one problem. He can't marry anybody within a year. Will you still be interested?" asked the Regidor.

"We have to be transparent with each other Cirilo. I think there is more to it," Don Julio questioned.

"Yes. My son will be married in two months. But he will become a widower shortly after. He is engaged to a young woman who is dying of typhus. She is the Duke of Leon's only daughter. You know what that means to have such a title. By marrying her, Santiago will be the first heir to the title. Now Julio, you must keep confidences. Santiago and I have other options if you decide otherwise," the Regidor cautioned.

"If it pleases you, it pleases me. As long as you don't say anything, I won't either," Don Julio replied.

"Let's finalize this agreement when I pay you a visit."

Both men shook hands and left to get ready for the social event. Don Julio was delighted to have such an opportunity.

"This is wonderful! My own daughter as a duchess! I couldn't ask for more," the Hacendado thought with a sigh full of satisfaction. He couldn't wait to see Ramon's face when the wedding announcement would be made public.

At the storage rooms, Fermín was annoyed to hear that Mariano was gone. The supervisor had searched for him all over the Hacienda but wasn't able to locate him. Fermín ordered to have Leonardo replace him, but the race champion had an assignment directly from Don Julio. When Fermín came to the stables to confront him, he hardly recognized him. Leonardo was dressed in a gray suit and a white shirt. His black leather boots contrasted his bulky silver bow tie. It was the only suit he had brought from La Casa Grande. Fermín resented his posture and elegance. He saw him as a direct opponent in the quest for Beatriz's affection.

"We need you at the storage house! Mariano is gone! Do you know where he is?" the man barked with a dry voice.

Leonardo immediately thought about the hidden rifle and Mariano's anger towards Don Julio. He wouldn't say a word to Fermín, but he would warn Beatriz.

"My stay here has ended. I'm not under Don Julio or you anymore," answered Leonardo. "I haven't seen Mariano since the day I left."

"What do you mean you are not under us?" Fermín inquired walking towards him.

"Yes. I came here to get ready for the University and I am ready. If I work, you will pay me but I have bigger priorities than counting your sacks," Leonardo countered.

Fermín didn't dare say anymore because he remembered the young man's origin. He also noticed a rifle by his bed. He left immediately. The time was short for his arenas of action to be illuminated.

In the main quarters, everyone was dressed up for the closing ceremony. The ballroom was already packed with aristocracy. They wanted to see Santiago's face when Beatriz danced with someone else.

Meanwhile, away from the Hacienda, a skinny figure found his way through the woods. He was sobbing and sweating as he rode a gray stubborn donkey. It was Mariano with a rifle in his hands. The terrible scene from his home was still playing in his mind. He had found the blacksmith shop burned to the ground and his family missing. The people around informed him that revolutionaries had taken over the small village, but the priest had also recognized Don Julio's men. He was blinded by a terrible hate and thirst for vengeance.

At the Hacienda, Fermín went directly to the kitchen after checking with his accomplices in the storage rooms. He needed to follow up on his main wild card. The man was already dressed as a waiter. He was to serve only Don Julio and the Regidor's table. Fermín would be supervising that table, too.

Beatriz had advised her maid to bring Leonardo into the patio as soon as she saw him. She was so relieved to know that he was alive, but now, she wanted some explanation. She walked down stairs and turned to the kitchen instead of the ballroom. She came to the patio and sat on the wooden bench. It was the same spot where Leonardo met her the first night he snuck into the Hacienda. She stood and sat down impatiently peeking down the corridor. She feared being found there by her father.

At the main entrance, Leonardo had to check in again with a second guard for security purposes. He had to sign a guestbook and then be escorted by an old, stern woman towards the ballroom. Some people whispered on the side when he walked through them with his head up. They recognized him as the champion and smiled when he nodded his head. When he was about to enter the gathering place, Martina called him and motioned for him to follow her. She took him to Beatriz.

"You are finally here!" Beatriz said taking a deep breath.

"You look beautiful," he replied taking her hand.

"We don't have much time, but you need to tell me what's going on between you and Elena!" Beatriz demanded.

"Elena? Nothing! There is nothing going on between us!" he replied, "Why do you ask in such a tone?"

"Please be truthful! I saw her sitting with you when I went to the storage rooms four days ago!"

"Out of her good heart, she brought me a meal. I couldn't be ungrateful! If I would have seen you, I would have invited you over. Besides, I was starving," he said making eye contact, "I am sorry that you thought something else was happening!"

"Are you really being honest with me?" Beatriz asked between a sob and a laugh.

"Yes! Absolutely! I need you to trust me!" begged Leonardo, "I see that such an idea caused you anguish. Why would I do such a foolish thing and hurt you? There are four treasures I would not trade for anything in the world; the joy in your smile, the brightness in your eyes, the warmth of your nature, and the freedom in your dreams."

Leonardo hugged her, and she surrendered to his arms feeling the healing power of love.

"I thought you were dead! I wanted to die too," she said in a sobbing voice.

"I'm glad you didn't die because I would've died too," he replied, "Who is this Santiago? Does he have a chance of stealing your heart from me?"

"Never! No one can," she answered, "let's talk to my father right now."

"What do we do if he refuses?" Leonardo asked.

"Let's hope he doesn't," she resolved.

"What if he locks you in or sends you away?" the young man asked.

"We will escape to California. We will need to get married first," Beatriz proposed, "I have some things packed already. Meet me at midnight, right below my window if necessary."

"Are you really saying what I hear? You are willing to run away with me? You must be sure of yourself," he asked.

"My freedom is dying and with it my life. I would rather be with the man I love and save future generations than live a life at the feet of tyrants," she explained. "Let's go! We need to be in there. Let me go ahead and you join me in a little bit." Beatriz whispered.

"Wait! I need to tell your father something terrible. Fermín is planning something against your family! We must warn Don Julio! You need to be very attentive!" he cautioned.

"You can tell him inside, I need to go!"

Leonardo remained behind. He was surprised to run into Fermín who was entering the hallway that connected the kitchen and the main entrance. The ruffian had a glass bottle with a dark liquid inside. He tried to hide it and walked away without saying a word. The young man commenced to approach the ballroom entrance.

A seat was reserved for him next to the main table. After greeting the others at the table, he learned that the lieutenant and the supervisor also shared his table. He immediately made eye contact with Beatriz who sat about five meters from him. He had made it just in time for dinner. After introductions at his table, he soon began to receive accolades about his triumph. The conversation was solely about the race. Leonardo embellished every aspect of his win, entertaining an enthusiastic crowd. He didn't stop glancing at Beatriz's table every other instant.

"How did you do it? I mean, winning in such a way. I heard that you entered the competition half an hour before," the man in uniform asked.

"First explain to us about defying Don Julio's decision not to race!" the supervisor interrupted.

"Don Julio allowed us to enter the race, so it wasn't against his will. Arnulfo, his horse tender had looked forward to it the whole year." Leonardo replied, "We just couldn't give up. I believed in my horse. Regardless of what the majority said or thought, I followed my intuition."

"But you were behind the whole race. How did you come in first?" the officer asked.

"I became aware of the rivalry between Eliodoro and the Regidor's son. I also knew that they both were first in the preliminary race. I just tried to follow close. Our horses were fast and full of stamina. The real difference was that my stallion knew I needed to win," the cowboy alleged.

"There seems to be a competition for Beatriz's heart. Will you win that race too?" the officer asked.

"You are just going to have to wait on that one," Leonardo replied.

Don Julio was also congratulated often for winning the race. Even the way he sat looked arrogant, but he wasn't too pleased to recognize Leonardo in public.

Right after dinner, the chilling sound of the trumpet called for everyone's attention.

"Ladies and gentlemen! Friends and family! We come to the close of a wonderful week," Don Julio announced, "It has been a week of celebration, competition, a week of selling, buying, and even dancing for some of you. Most of all, it has been a time to enjoy the company of friends. We hope you liked your stay here. At this time, I want to introduce our Regidor, Cirilo Del Castillo!"

"Good evening! It is wonderful to be here. I would like you to join me in giving a hand to the Cortez Family for their hospitality. Thank you Julio, Mrs. Cortez, Beatriz. It's been great!" the Regidor said, "I confess it was hard to accept an invitation away from Guanajuato, especially, with people whom I didn't know. But now, I feel at home. Thanks again."

The audience cheered and clapped at the end of his words. The Regidor and Don Julio walked to the middle of the hall and took medals from a silver tray.

"At this time we will confer medals upon our winners," Don Julio announced.

He called them in order from sixth to first place. Eleodoro sent his younger brother to receive his medal. As soon as Santiago took his medal, he clapped pointing at Leonardo. It was a tradition that the first runner up would present the medal to the winner. The whole ballroom erupted with clamor. "Leonardo! Leonardo!" they called.

After he walked towards them and received his medal, he raised his hands and took a bow. A total of seven men including the Regidor and Don Julio shook his hand. After the laurel crown was carefully placed on his head and he was pronounced the champion, he took another bow. He then took the carnation that had been pinned to his jacket and presented it to Beatriz. She loved and admired him. The grin on her face reflected the consent and satisfaction to see him. As soon as he returned to his table, Don Julio addressed the people again.

"Let's continue with the tradition! Will the Hacendado's and their wives join us for the waltz?"

Ramon and his wife were the first ones to get to the dance floor. The man turned to Don Julio and to the Regidor.

"Allow me, please! Leonardo will you invite any fine lady to join us on the floor!" Ramon called in a loud voice.

Leonardo knew exactly whom to ask. Beatriz got up even before he got to her table. Aristocracy's tongue moved like a snake while the elite danced. Some pitied Santiago, others laughed at him. Some admired the new couple, but others complained about Leonardo's social class. Santiago kept drinking cold water. He looked at Eleodoro as if he were the man to beat. His intentions were to take Beatriz to the garden right after the waltz. Eleodoro put on a scornful smile every time he looked at Santiago. He seemed to be enjoying Santiago's jealousy even though he felt the same way.

In the middle of the floor, Leonardo and Beatriz danced as if in a dream. They looked nowhere else but at each other. Then at the door, Fermín showed up with a tray in his hands. It had several cups and a bottle. Three spoons were also placed on top of a white cloth. He signaled to the waiter who tended Don Julio's table. The bottle was a mixture of some kind of red liquor and rattle snake venom.

"We become part of history tonight! Can you imagine General Allende's face when I tell him we took care of Don Julio and the Regidor? He will appoint me as one of his chief men and you; you are coming with me! Go and deliver the definite blow but remember, do not to serve any to Don Julio's daughter!" Fermín advised the waiter.

The man walked towards the main table and stood there until the dancing was over. He held the tray without serving.

On the dance floor, Leonardo and Beatriz couldn't wait to talk to Don Julio about their romance but they figured it wasn't the right time. They both decided to enjoy the evening there. The music ended, so everyone returned to their seats. When the Regidor saw the red bottle, he indicated to the waiter to serve him.

"This one has been especially reserved for the toast Sir. But try this other," The waiter replied.

Cirilo was displeased. He looked to an astounded Don Julio.

"Let's have the toast right away!" the Regidor suggested.

Don Julio motioned for the trumpet to call everyone's attention. He then motioned for the waiter to serve them.

"Ladies and gentlemen, please give me your attention. At this time, please join us in a toast. Let's do it as a symbol of our friendship, our success in New Spain, and long live the King of Spain!" Don Julio said extending his cup to be filled with the red liquid. All the audience erupted in cheers, then suddenly, a loud scratchy voice caught everyone's attention.

"DON JULIO CORTEZ! YOU WILL PAY FOR ALL YOUR CRIMES! PREPARE TO DIE!"

It was Mariano pointing his weapon from across the ballroom.

"You ordered your men to murder my parents, and now you will pay for it!" the blacksmith shouted as his trembling hands aimed at the main table."

"MARIANO! Wait! Don't shoot!" cried Leonardo trying to distract him.

Without any more words, two lead balls were fired. The last one came from Fermín and impacted Mariano's back. The first one came from Mariano's bayonet and hit the waiter who stood holding the tray next to Don Julio. Everything was spilled on the floor. Everyone stood still in shock. Don Julio promptly led the Regidor and his family out into his office. The other Hacendados followed behind. The celebration was crashed by the army who took control of the house. Don Julio opened his arsenal and gave a pistol to every man in his office. Everything happened so fast that no one saw what had happened to Beatriz.

"Beatriz! Beatriz! Is my daughter here?" Don Julio's wife cried.

"Let's go find her!" shouted Santiago.

"No, you stay here and let her father and the lieutenant go find her," the Regidor ordered.

He tried to stop him, but the bachelor pushed his way through the crowded room and left.

Don Julio asked the soldiers if they had seen his daughter as he ran towards the hall.

"Come on Santiago and Eleodoro! Let's check in her chamber upstairs!" Don Julio commanded while catching his breath.

"I saw Fermín taking her!" explained one of the soldiers pointing down the hall to the kitchen.

Once they got to the kitchen, they found an unconscious man on the ground just outside the door. It was Fermín. When they noticed that he was breathing, they dragged him inside the room. He had a broken nose and a cut on his eyebrow.

"WHERE IS MY DAUGHTER?" Don Julio roared.

"Leonardo abducted her! I tried to stop him, but I was attacked from behind! He has accomplices! He planned this attack, and we must stop him now before he escapes!" Fermín explained.

"What are you talking about? He planned what?" demanded Don Julio.

"Yes! Leonardo joined the rebels during the round up. He and Mariano are only bait!" explained Fermín.

"LOOK! The storage rooms are on fire!"

"Oh heavens! Where is the army? Why aren't they protecting us?" Don Julio cried, "Fermín, we must put the fire out. Gather all the men! Eleodoro! Go with Fermín and check the stables. Beatriz might be with Leonardo there?"

Don Julio and Santiago went back to the house and checked every room upstairs. Don Julio went straight to Beatriz' chamber while Santiago checked all the other rooms. There was a brown leather bag on the bed with Beatriz' clothes inside. The Hacendado's face revealed his fear. The very thought that his own daughter was planning to run away broke his heart. Inside the bag, there was the letter Beatriz had written for her mother. His thoughts became reality when he read it. His daughter expressed her love and a clear declaration of independence.

"I can't believe it! My own daughter wants to leave!" he cried out loud without noticing Santiago at the door. "Whoever brain washed her will pay with his life!"

"She is planning to run away?" Santiago questioned.

Don Julio couldn't hide the evidence. He put the letter in his pocket and took out his pistol.

"Let's find that Leonardo! I will send him to the mines!" Don Julio denounced.

Both men were met by the Regidor and Ramon at the main entrance. The entire Hacienda was under siege by the army.

"We have control of the situation!" the Regidor cried, "Two men have been captured and confessed to Fermín that Leonardo is the brain of this attempt."

"Where is my daughter? We need to find my daughter!" Don Julio howled heading for the stables.

The fire was under control at the storage rooms, but half of the stables were burned down.

Men ran fetching water from a cement pool by the stables. Others had gone all the way to the lagoon. Through the smog, Don Julio was able to confirm his thoughts again. The white stallion was missing, and no one knew where it was.

"After the race, I took the stallion to the main quarters through the back. Leonardo told me that people would want to see it." Miguel explained.

"That was such an idiotic thing to do!" Don Julio railed.

"Prepare the horses! They can't be far! I will go south with my men. I beg you! Please help me find her!" Don Julio told the Lieutenant, "She has been taken captive."

Fugitives

Four expedition teams were formed. Don Julio immediately offered a rich reward for anyone who would find Beatriz. Ramon and Eleodoro headed north, and Miguel and his cowboys marched west. Santiago was exasperated and quickly joined a search squad. His father was not pleased to see him react that way. He knew his son was an appealing target for any revolutionaries.

About three kilometers south of Cieneguilla, two riders moved in the dark. The sound of their horse's hooves against the brush revealed the rush. Beatriz rode the white colt and Leonardo a black thoroughbred stallion. They could still hear the turmoil at the Hacienda. They were on their way to Teocaltiche to find Patricio, the priest. He had promised to help Leonardo reach California.

The fugitives were afraid to be captured, but they were joyful to be together. Leonardo didn't know the way, so he had to return to the main road once in a while. He knew that was the only way to get to town. There was no better opportunity to run away than this one. They just needed to get directions from the priest. From there, they would stop at La Casa Grande and then head north for a month.

Just at the outskirts of Don Julio's property, a group of men headed in the same direction. It was Don Julio,

Santiago, Fermín, the Lieutenant, and ten soldiers. The barking of their dogs scared away the owls on the fences.

"I have the order here with me. As soon as we catch that bandit, he becomes indentured! Of course, I will give him a beating first!" Don Julio threatened, "I have a feeling he is headed for Teocaltiche. That's the only place he knows. We will go there first and then to La Casa Grande."

"My race stallion is missing! If he took it, I will make him a capital prisoner!" Santiago whined, "That adds a few years working in the mines or prison!"

"If he took the girl by force, he is worthy of capital punishment!" the Lieutenant explained.

"Of course he did! He probably threatened to kill her or her loved ones if she didn't comply!" denounced Don Julio.

"Then we better trap them soon. They can't be far if they're headed in this direction," Fermín said.

The pursuit went on all night long. Dawn was threatening to uncover the night and thus favoring the pursuers. Leonardo and Beatriz were exhausted. They could not go any further. Just when they were about to rest by some bushes, two distant towers fueled their will to go on. It was Teaocaltiche, the same town where Mariano's parents ran the blacksmith shop. They made it at a perfect time when everyone was sound asleep. They reached the wheat mill in town which was a few lots before Mariano's home. Leonardo was shocked to see the barren walls and a pile of ashes. It used to be the blacksmith shop, and now, only piles of ashes and smoke remained.

"Something terrible has happened! Mariano's parents used to live here. That explains why he rushed in anger against your father!" Leonardo said.

"But I don't think my father ordered someone to do such an awful thing," Beatriz answered.

"I think Fermín is behind all this," he explained, "I told you already, I heard him say he was going to overthrow your father."

"But why did he try to force me to come with him? He dragged me to the kitchen. He tried to kiss me! I got hold of a clay jar and smashed his face," Beatriz recollected feeling goose bumps all over.

"Somehow he found out you and I knew about his plans. That's why his abettors are chasing us," Leonardo concluded.

"But why would they try to kill us?" Beatriz asked, "They fired at us. They knew it was me, the Hacendado's daughter!"

"He figured that I told you already," he said.

"Who will protect us until my father comes to rescue us?" she asked in a worried tone,

"What if they hurt my parents?"

"Everyone knows your father in this town. There has to be a commissioner for the peace,"

Leonardo replied, "I was hoping Zenón would help us, but I am sure the priest will."

"Do you think they are still following us all the way here?" she asked, "maybe we should've run inside the Hacienda." Beatriz lamented.

"But you saw that they were shooting at us. We would have been killed," replied Leonardo, "Let's wait for your father. Don't worry, everything will be alright. I will talk to Don Julio about us when everything is cleared."

The two riders continued all the way to the church building. There was a door through the side, but Leonardo knew he needed to hide the horses. A watchman opened a small window on the wooden door.

"Is this an emergency? You need to wait until the morning."

"Please! We need to see Father Patricio! Don Julio's daughter is here with me!" Leonardo insisted until the sleepy guard agreed to let them into the stable behind the structure. He sent them all the way around the other side of the building. Once there, they found a barb wire corral with a post to tie their beasts. Their feet were so numb that they could hardly walk. Adjacent to the wall, there was a small storage room with some hay and tools. Leonardo arranged the hay in such a way that it covered the dusty floor. Without much thought, both riders sat down and quickly fell asleep. Fermín's plan to take over the Hacienda had failed but now he blamed Leonardo for his failed attempt. The crook was determined to eliminate the young cowboy.

About two hours later, the couple was awakened by the priest. He took them inside his house behind the church building. Beatriz fell asleep as soon as she lay down in a guest room. Leonardo quickly informed Patricio about Fermín's threat and actions. They both left immediately to notify the commissioner in town.

"Have you heard who betrayed your father?" asked the priest.

"No, do you know anything about it?" Leonardo asked with great interest.

"Not yet but how much did he tell you about his last assignment?"

"Not much, he gave me more advice than usual," the cowboy answered.

"Are you aware that he objected to the vice-royalty's heavy taxing and the Mestizo's exploitation?" Patricio asked.

"You can trust me as much as you trusted him. My father and I had no secrets," Leonardo said.

"What kind of advice did he give you?" the priest asked carefully watching his words. He needed to be sure Leonardo was aware of the secret movement to establish freedom in the land.

"What else do you know about General Ignacio Allende and Aldama?" the cowboy asked trying to trap him in words.

"Look Leonardo, I was there when your father joined them. I know everything!" the priest said in a whisper. "Do you know what I mean?"

"Yes, I am supposed to join the cause when it breaks out," he answered.

"We must be very careful about this. You will not join any cause! Your family already lost the head figure. Your father has done more than enough. He gave his life. I promised your father that I would send you far away from here. I will do that tonight!" Patricio said in a commanding tone.

"Do you mean California?" asked Leonardo. "I need to bring Beatriz with me."

"That's impossible! It will be twice as hard to hide her; plus imagine the witch hunt, Don Julio and the government will search even under the rocks. No way! It would be too risky!"

"I will not leave without her!" the cowboy affirmed.

When they reached the commissioner's house, he was still asleep. He was quite annoyed to be awakened so early. But then, he was grateful and worried after he heard Leonardo repeat the whole incident again.

"After the blacksmith shop was burned down and some stores vandalized, I asked for help from my superiors. To this day, I am still waiting for reinforcements from Guadalajara, the capital city," the officer explained.

Leonardo and the priest left his house relieved that some guards would be posted on the outskirts. It was too late because as soon as they walked ten meters towards the cathedral, Leonardo was seized by a squad on horses. The Vallejo kid was astonished to see the soldiers pointing their weapons at him, but felt some relief when he recognized Don Julio.

"STOP RIGHT THERE! WE WILL SHOOT IF YOU MOVE!" the Lieutenant roared.

"WHERE IS MY DAUGHTER?" cried Don Julio trapping them with his horse. "What have you done to her?"

"Nothing! She is safe!" Leonardo answered realizing the misunderstanding. "HE IS THE REAL THREAT!" he shouted pointing to Fermín who was getting off his horse.

Fermín delivered a punch to his stomach before he could say anymore. He was interrupted by Santiago who lifted Leonardo and pushed him against an adobe wall.

"ANSWER THE QUESTION! WHERE IS BEATRIZ?"

Santiago held him by the shirt against the wall. Leonardo extended his right hand over his left hand and poked his eye. The cowboy was about to punch him when a rider attacked him. It was Don Julio who lifted his whip and lashed Leonardo's shoulder. The Vallejo kid fell on one knee only to receive three more hits on his back.

The priest got in between and interceded for the young man.

"She is fine! She is in my house! Leave him alone! Julio what is happening here?"

"Tie him up and take him to jail! Make sure he is well guarded!" howled Don Julio turning to the soldiers.

Leonardo kept on claiming his innocence out loud. He also assured Don Julio that he was wrong about Fermín.

"Leonardo is a traitor! He abducted my daughter! He tried to murder everyone in the Hacienda!" Don Julio hollered.

"Take me to Beatriz!" he requested turning to the priest.

"That's not what he told me! You have to hear what he saw and heard," the priest claimed.

"There is no time to lose! Take us to Beatriz right away!" Santiago demanded.

The priest motioned for them to follow him to his house. Don Julio sent Fermín and five of the soldiers to safeguard Leonardo. The others accompanied him to the church. Once there, Don Julio asked everyone to wait outside the bedroom. He locked the door behind him.

"Beatriz! Beatriz! Wake up!" he called moving his daughter gently.

"Papa, Oh father! I am so happy to see you!" the young woman answered back jumping to his arms.

"Are you hurt? Did he do anything to you?" he asked.

"I'm fine. Where is Leonardo? Fermín's men were chasing us! They tried to kill us! Fermín has betrayed you! He tried to take me hostage, but I broke away. I had to hit him with a vase because he wouldn't let me go! We must take every precaution!" Beatriz explained as she cleaned her tears.

"Listen carefully; I know the truth! I know that you were planning to run away with that turkey! I read your note in the bag. Fermín was trying to protect you. I know Leonardo can be deceiving, and he almost got away with it. You made a terrible mistake! Tell me, where can you go? What will he offer you? He is a nobody! He will pay for this! He and Mariano tried to murder me!"

"No father! That isn't true! He tried to stop Mariano! He did not convince me! It was you, your unrighteous dominion, and your greediness for gold that convinced me to leave," Beatriz revealed.

"Nonsense! You have almost ruined our only chance to live a worthy future! I command you to stop your nonsense right now! You will tell everyone that he forced you to leave! You will say that he pointed a gun at you and threatened to kill your family if you didn't comply," Don Julio ordered. "Better yet, I will do all the explaining! You will remain silent about the incident. Never mention a word to your mother! You know the grief and disappointment you will cause. I will burn your letter! Is that understood? Is that understood?" Don Julio demanded.

"I will not comply with your desires!" Beatriz answered.

Don Julio lost control and slapped his daughter. The long ride and the sleepless night was no excuse for the physical and emotional abuse to his daughter. Such was the fate for women, in a dark era, in the history of people.

Santiago knocked on the door. He was eager to see Beatriz. Don Julio let him in when he walked out to the living room. It was then that he signed the order to send Leonardo to the mines. He interfered so much with his plans. Keeping him away from Beatriz' life was the best way to open the way for Santiago.

"Lieutenant! Deliver our prisoner to the Guanajuato commissioner! The Regidor has already signed the form and now, I second his decree. You can do with him as he deserves or as you please. I don't want to see him again!"

The Lieutenant took the paper and gave it to his sergeant who immediately went to the town jail. The officer then hinted to the priest to have breakfast prepared while Don Julio and Santiago discussed what happened. Beatriz remained locked in the bedroom. As soon as everyone finished eating, they all took a nap to prepare for the trip back. Father Patricio took advantage of the opportunity and interviewed Beatriz about the matter. His instinct was right. Fermín was behind all the lies, and Leonardo was innocent. It was too late; the sergeant and his squad were already on their way to the town jail. They would take Leonardo to Guanajuato.

In the afternoon, Don Julio and Santiago were ready to go home. Fermín was back to report on his assignment.

"It would be better that I continue on to Guanajuato. I believe that you should join our family as soon as possible. It would be more relaxing after such an unpleasant incident," Santiago suggested.

"I will come as soon as I put everything in order at the Hacienda. What did my daughter tell you?" Don Julio asked.

"She didn't need to say a word. All she needed was a hug and comfort. She ran to my arms when she saw me." Santiago explained fully adorning Beatriz's cold greeting. "Don't take it wrong. But I am really fond of your daughter. I understand it is my father's place to ask, but…I would like to marry your daughter as soon as you consent to it."

"I am glad to hear that. You will be a worthy husband. She is the best there is. I will be pleased to fulfill your desire," Don Julio answered, "in that case, I will come to Guanajuato in three days."

Both men embraced each other and walked out towards the back of the building. They found the two stallions tied to a post.

"I am pleased to find my horse safe. What will you do with that one?" asked Santiago pointing to Lightning.

"That's Beatriz' horse and soon to be yours, too," Don Julio answered.

"Wonderful! Do you mind if I take it to Guanajuato? This is the only horse that has outrun mine," the Bachelor asked.

"Take it, I never liked it at all," the Hacendado answered.

A carriage was prepared to take Don Julio and his daughter back to his quarters. Fermín was already sitting with the driver. When they were about to part, a familiar company of five stagecoaches approached the cathedral. It was the Regidor and his people and Don Julio's wife traveling with them. The Regidor ran to greet Santiago as soon as he saw him. Mrs. Cortez also ran to embrace Beatriz. Both women cried like little children. It was then that Santiago insisted on ending his life as a bachelor.

"Father, I need to speak to you in private," Santiago said leading his father inside the church building, "I have found that true love is greater that titles and riches. I have decided to break my promise to the Duke of Leon. Marriage deserves seriousness, a total commitment from both parties.

I don't feel anything but pity for his daughter. Such a marriage would be for the wrong reason."

"What are you saying? It is for a good reason! You will make this woman happy for the rest of her short life. It speaks well of you. That is true love," his father replied, "is there something else?"

"The truth is that I can't live another minute without Beatriz. I want her by my side every moment," Santiago said.

The Regidor looked around. All he found was the altar deep beyond and a St. Martin statue with burned candles on his right. He wouldn't dare say a filthy word in such a place.

"I already spoke to her father. Don Julio has agreed to our marriage next week," Santiago said trying to close all options for a comeback from his father.

"Next week? You want to get married next week? Are you out of your mind?" Cirilo questioned with distress.

"Love and luck are on my side. That's what I desire to do. Please grant me your approval father," Santiago replied in a begging tone.

"Let's give it some thought and consideration. You have the chance to be appointed Duke of Leon. It will give you all the influence and prestige a man can dream of. You are letting this opportunity pass only to be with a rebellious pretty face. Come on! Anybody in his right mind can see it is a mistake," the Regidor argued.

"I will do it with or without your approval! I would very much like to have your consent," Santiago declared in a respectful way.

Cirilo walked out of the church building. He went straight to his coach and gave orders get ready to continue their trip back to Guanajuato. Don Julio came and thanked him for all his assistance. "I apologize for such an unpleasant experience last night. I promise I will make it up to you. I am still planning to come to your place in three days to finalize our agreement if that pleases you."

"Where is our prisoner?" the Regidor asked.

"He was taken into custody. The escort left for Guanajuato about twenty minutes before you got here," Don Julio replied, "The order was signed. He will be punished according to his crimes."

"Capital punishment?" the Regidor continued.

"He deserves it! He will be assigned to the mines, but you may do with him as you desire," Don Julio said.

From inside the carriage, Cirilo stared at Beatriz who stood next to her father. He was trying to reason out his son's feelings for her. Just in that moment, Beatriz broke away grabbing the black stallion that was tied to the carriage. She brought it close to Cirilo's carriage and by stepping on the axle mounted the beast. Everything happened so fast that by the time they reacted, she was already past the cathedral.

"BEATRIZ! STOP!" cried her mother.

"She can't go far. She is not a good rider!" yelled Don Julio, signaling to Fermín to go after her, then turning to his wife with disappointment.

He expected her to convince Beatriz to change her mind. The first on horseback was Santiago. He caught up to Beatriz right at the end of town. With an efficient reach, he grabbed her horse's reign and forced the animal to stop.

"Let me go! Let me go! I need to save Leonardo!" she cried.

"I give you my word! I will spare his life!" Santiago promised, "Come on! Let's go back to our parents. It's better that you let us deal with it."

"You have to believe me! Leonardo was trying to protect me from Fermín!" cried the woman.

"Fermín is plotting to kill my parents and take over the Hacienda!"

"Are you sure of that? How do you know?" Santiago asked.

"He ordered his men to burn the storage rooms and the stables! He tried to kidnap me during the dance. If it wasn't for Leonardo, I would have been killed. His men even fired their guns at us!" Beatriz explained.

Just then, Fermín arrived and commanded the girl to come to her parents. He got off his horse and threw his lasso on the black stallion. Santiago calculated the man's movements trying to confirm Beatriz's words.

"Don't leave me alone with him!" the young woman begged extending her hand to Santiago.

"I will take care of it. Here! Take my horse Fermín," Santiago demanded as he dismounted and handed his horse to the man.

He mounted with Beatriz and turned the stallion around back to their parents.

"Leonardo has been arrested; he will be tried and hanged. Only my father and I can stop it," Santiago explained.

"Do so, please! He is innocent!" Beatriz interrupted.

"I want to make you a proposition. Your life for his life," he said.

"What do you mean?" she asked.

"If you agree to live your life as my wife, I will let Leonardo live," he said without the intent of keeping his promise.

"I would need to see him free," Beatriz agreed feeling that her sacrifice was smaller than her love for Leonardo.

Don Julio's anger was soon dispelled when he contemplated Santiago and his daughter riding together. Cirilo had no choice than to accept what he was witnessing. Even Cirilo's wife suggested that Beatriz had planned this incident so her son would run after her.

"You gave me your word. You will help Leonardo! I need to come to Guanajuato," Beatriz demanded.

"You have to come to Guanajuato with us. Your parents can join us later," the bachelor suggested.

When they arrived back with the company, Don Julio helped her down and escorted her inside his carriage. Mrs. Cortez also boarded. Beatriz tried to explain Fermín's plans, but they didn't listen. At the same time, Santiago convinced his father to allow the Cortez Family to come along with them. The Regidor came to Don Julio's stagecoach and gave recommendations.

"Julio, my son has just learned from your daughter, that there is a great threat at your quarters. There is a conspiracy to take over the estate. Your lives are in peril! I advise you to stay away until more Realist troops reinforce this area. If you don't mind, I would like you to come with us for a while. It is safer!"

Don Julio looked at Beatriz. She agreed right away.

"You need to tell me everything you know!" demanded Don Julio.

"I already told you, but you did not believe me," Beatriz answered.

"Come on Julio! I have plenty of room in my house. We can use this time to take care of business. Antonio will arrive tomorrow," the Regidor proposed.

Everyone agreed to leave for Guanajuato except Fermín. He was ordered by Don Julio to go back to the Hacienda and put down any rebellion there. Don Julio also advised him to join him in Guanajuato in two days. The boss wanted a full report about the estate conditions. Fermín was delighted to hear that. This time, he was going to finish the job. He would have plenty of time to adjust his plans.

Several miles ahead, a cavalry of five soldiers escorted a caged wagon.

Inside, a weak Leonardo had his feet and hands tied. He had a dirty bandana tied around his eyes and another in his mouth. The group stopped at San Juan de los Lagos for food. From there, it would be another day of travel until the Guanajuato outskirts. The prisoner was hungry and thirsty. The wounds on his shoulder and back hurt like a burn. He was reflecting on his situation. The thought of his father's death sank him into depression. It was then that his mother's distant words came to him.

"Pray for strength, pray for protection, pray for wisdom."

It was like a whisper that came with the wind and caressed his hair. As he lifted his head, he was astonished to see his hands free. There was no guard, he was untied and standing on his feet. He looked in every direction, fearing that he was the target for the hidden soldiers. He found himself in the middle of a yellow, grassy field, not knowing where to go. He advanced to a barbwire fence several feet from him. Once he cleared the spikes, he saw a sturdy mesquite tree in the middle of the field. Tripping a few times but getting up, he hurried until reaching temporary safety behind the tree. The cowboy sensed he was being watched, but he couldn't see anyone. After sitting for a moment, he recognized the creek a hundred meters from the tree.

"I know they're hiding in the creek. I am afraid I will run into them? But I can't stay here!"

He rested his head on the trunk and sat back. Seconds later, he got up and dashed directly to the creek. Precisely when he was in the open field, a horrible creature charged right behind him. It was a Charolais bull, pushing fire through his nostrils. Leonardo's weak, slow legs were no match for the beast's potent strides. His sharp horns advanced closer and closer, almost tearing Leonardo's shirt. Running for his life, he got tangled in a shrub and fell on his face. The bull jumped over him just missing his shoulder. The cowboy knew the creek was his only chance, so he ran almost flying over the ground. The terrible beast was right behind him.

"It's over! My lungs will explode! My legs can't go any further!"

Suddenly, the ground disappeared under him, and he soared in the air. The creek was really a cliff. The sight of the raging bull, at the top of the precipice, kept him unaware of the unknown bottom. It was too late to remember that he couldn't swim. The cold piercing water revived his adrenaline. He kicked and swung desperately, trying to come back to the surface. It was useless; he kept sinking to the bottom. His head felt the water pressure, and his vision faded from blurry to black. Right when he was about to give up and sink into death, he heard a familiar voice.

"Leonardo! Leonardo!" the voice hummed.

"Is this it? Am I dead already?" he thought.

"No, not yet. It isn't your time. Fight back! Live!"

Leonardo vividly recognized his mother's image extending her hand to help him.

"Mama! Mama! Where are you?" he cried.

The soldier's loud laughter woke him up from his delirious vision.

"He is a cry baby! Did you hear him call his mama?" one of the soldiers mocked.

Leonardo didn't know which was worst, his reality, his dream, or even waking up from it. It was a literal communication from the other side of the veil. His mother's voice reminded him of her last recorded words in a treasured letter. She wrote it before she died. They were words of encouragement which reflecting a plea from past generations. He read them often and guarded that letter like a precious jewel. Those words came to his heart.

My dear child,

Like a gliding eagle captures its prey, this new adversary on my flesh is taking my life.

The wise medicine healers with their hundred herbs and unbreakable faith, are powerless to the quick effect of this foreign sting.

Such new illnesses have been the real cause for past generations' disappearance.

I know my fate. Death will pass over me like an evening with an invisible wind.

My tears, my sorrow, my longing to be with you become pleadings to the Great Spirit.

His peace has calmed my soul at dawn. I am not scared!

Just sad for the premature parting. Sad to miss your soft and tender kisses, heartbroken to let go of your hand.

Go my son! Don't be scared. Go on and fulfill your purpose in the land.

Hold on to the freedom the Great Spirit gave the sparrow, walk freely through the woods.

Respect the trees, the jaguar, and the river.

The grand chiefs of the past foresaw your day.

Endure the tribulations, endure the chastisement, trials will give you experience and strength.

Yes, the necessary wisdom for your children's children to blossom in barren desolation like a flower.

Farewell for now, wherever you go, I will always be watching over you.

Your mother,
Techiayotl

His will to go on was renewed. Even though his situation was obscure, he hoped to find justice in Guanajuato. He was hoping to have an audience with the Corregidor.

When the company entered the next small town, the officer in charge learned of the terrible events around the neighboring towns. The struggle for independence had begun the previous week. The soldiers learned that all the northwest territory was controlled by the insurgent army led by the priest Miguel Hidalgo. Scared to fall to their hands, the sergeant continued on his way to Guanajuato going east, avoiding the small township in the vicinity.

At the Hacienda, Arnulfo had his own battle with death. He had lost too much blood. He was burning with fever. Miguel was back with a doctor from Aguascalientes. The administrator had placed men all over to guard the Hacienda. The other search squads had returned. Once the remaining soldiers returned, they took the horses from the corral and left Don Julio's quarters on their way to Guanajuato. On the road, they met Fermín and he explained the good news.

"Beatriz has been rescued. She is now with her parents. Leonardo was taken into custody. He will receive punishment according to his crime. Thank you for all your help."

"What about the rest of the army? Where are they heading now?" The officer in charge brought up.

"The Lieutenant wants you to join him in Guanajuato as soon as possible. If you hurry, you will catch up with them right before they arrive," Fermín advised with the intent to send them far away from the Hacienda.

Don Julio, Cirilo, and company made their stop at San Juan too. They spent the night and left after breakfast.

"We must be watchful all the way! We are in enemy territory. The innkeeper informed me that rebels took over a town not far from here!" Don Julio explained.

"They will not attack the Regidor; these twenty soldiers will quickly put them down, right? Santiago posed.

"They are still dangerous, they hide in the canyons and fire from afar," advised the Lieutenant, "Let's leave at once!"

About one hundred kilometers east, the small troop that escorted Leonardo went through the town of Dolores. It was almost a ghost town, occupied mostly by women and children. Ten days ago, the chime of church bells had initiated a major turning point in the land. The local parishioner assembled an army of peasants and took control of the neighboring towns. Today, the people in the village were quiet and watchful. They stared at the traveling company with hatred. The soldiers feared a surprise attack. They were nervous because a mob began to follow them. They threatened to attack with sticks and stones if they didn't free the prisoner.

"Let him go! Let him go!" the mob cried, "Libertad, Justicia!"

The sergeant knew they should have gone around the city, but that would have taken two hours longer. He fired his musket in the air trying to scare them away, but that didn't work. Once outside of town, the mob threw rocks hitting two soldiers. It was then that they fired back killing a few in the crowd.

Through the cage bars, Leonardo felt the warm September sun on his head. He was aware of the war breakout that happened ten days before. That time when he was taken prisoner during the round up, gave him a better notion of the revolution. He learned that a secret movement to free the land and proclaim equal rights had been discovered in the neighboring region of Queretaro. Insurgent forces fought openly for independence. For him, it was not a reality yet, since his captors only allowed him to eat once.

Far behind, Beatriz felt the same sun through a small window in the carriage. She didn't stop looking ahead, hoping to catch up with the prisoner. She repeated the entire story to her parents, expecting them to empathize with Leonardo, but it was useless. She was submitted to a deep questioning about her moral principles. Time after time, she claimed and explained her innocence. She defended Leonardo with all her might and words. It was then that Don Julio broke the news about his marriage consent.

"I have consented for Santiago Del Castillo to take you as his wife."

"Father please! I beg you! Don't do that to me! How can you force your only child to such misery?" the young woman cried. "Don't you have any love for me?"

Don Julio stared at her and silently choked in his response. For the first time, he felt a thread of guilt in his chest. His sobbing wife was not an option for back up or comfort.

"You will thank us later!" he grumbled.

"Beatriz! Any man you marry besides Santiago will make you miserable anyway!" her mother said, "Just do what your father and mother think is best for you."

Beatriz remembered her pact with Santiago and imagined her life by his side. Her mother's words expressed some disappointment with her own marriage herself.

Back at the Hacienda, Fermín had taken over the leadership. He made sure his most loyal conspirators were assigned to key positions. He had also put down a farmer revolt outside the burned storage rooms. Peasants had taken most of the grain that was saved. They had also seized and killed some cattle. They were dispersed by force, and identified ring leaders were executed in public. Fermín appointed the supervisor as his right hand. He also placed guards on the main road to keep an eye on travelers and visitors to the property. Part of his plan was to stop Don Julio from returning. He placed a mercenary in the woods near the road. His intention was to eliminate the Cortez Family when they returned. The crook planned to leave for Guanajuato to bring luggage and silver. He decided to do it because he still wanted to bring Beatriz to Cieneguilla. He was determined to do it by force, and to eliminate anybody who got in his way.

Guanajuato

The midday sun sparkled on the rocky soil, revealing the disorderly colonized canyon along the waterless river. The northeastern part of the narrow valley was full of buildings where aristocracy and mine owners built their fortresses. Their majestic castles adorned the top of the hills, but the city was a total contrast. Poor farmers had built their homes in shacks and caves. All structures had been built on peasants' backs; nevertheless, poverty banned them from dwelling in luxurious places. The Valenciana Mine was at its height. More than half the silver in the world had been extracted from there. Nonetheless, Leonardo would be forced to work at the Moreno pit, near the Mellado Mine, on the west south side of the city.

The soldiers felt safer once they approached downtown and saw the Alhondiga. The enormous granite fortress stood out among the other constructions. Once they arrived, the prisoner was put in a cell until the Audiencia came in session. Leonardo was finally fed for the day and his eyes and mouth liberated.

Four hours later, the Regidor and Don Julio arrived in the city. Santiago remained behind the city's entrance where he had a bigger stable. The Regidor's quarters were on the east side of town; nevertheless, he had to report to the Alhóndiga. He was asked about the prisoner, but he only directed them to his signed order. Don Julio wanted to make sure Leonardo was behind bars, so he asked to see the prisoner. Once he was led into Leonardo's cell, he grabbed him and threw him into a corner.

"You will tell me the truth! Who is behind all this? Who planned the attack? ANSWER ME!"

"It is Fermín! You have to believe me! He wants to kill you and your family!" Leonardo replied.

"What makes you say that?"

"I heard his plans the night you were away! Your men have betrayed you! They plotted the attack!" Leonardo declared, "They burned down the smith shop. I am innocent! You can ask Beatriz! She knows they tried to kill us! Bring her here, and she will repeat the same thing!"

Hearing Leonardo say his daughter's name irritated the Hacendado. It was then that he reacted defensively.

"Don't mention my daughter! She has nothing to do with it. You planned to take her away from me, then again, you failed! Thanks to Santiago, she has come to her senses. They will get married tomorrow!"

His words came like a dagger to his heart. He figured Beatriz was being forced to get married just like she feared.

"You will make her miserable! She doesn't love Santiago! She loves me!"

The Hacendado felt defeated to hear those words because he remembered Beatriz' letter. His response broke the young man's spirit.

"She can never love you! You are no one! You are a heathen, fatherless criminal who will die just like your father did. He betrayed the Crown, his class, and race!

"My father was no traitor because he didn't see a difference between races. Closed minded men like you judge only what your eyes see! My father judged the hearts of men!" Leonardo responded in a sob.

"What do you know about feelings of the heart? I can only feel pity for you! That's something that your father's brother, Antonio, can't feel. He hates you! That's why he took your inheritance! He and I knew about the insurgent movement and didn't warn your father!

"So you know who killed my father! Did you kill my father? Answer me! Who killed my father?" Leonardo demanded. "Did Antonio kill my father?"

"I wasn't involved!" Don Julio answered.

"Please don't leave me here! DON'T LEAVE ME HERE!" Leonardo cried as Don Julio vanished in the dark.

Don Julio had second thoughts about his men. The Regidor had advised him to stay away from Fermín until he was captured and interrogated. Leaving Leonardo there was a perfect strategy to keep him from interfering in Beatriz and Santiago's wedding.

The company left the fortress, and continued east past the San Diego Cathedral, which was adjacent to Cirilo del Castillo's house. Soon, they stopped in front of the mansion. Before entering the two story house, Beatriz walked to a little plaza near the entrance. She looked around trying to figure out an escape route. Her only alternative was a balcony in the west side of the house. There was a second balcony in the neighbor's residence, about one meter away. It would be easy to jump from balcony to balcony.

Back at the Alhondiga, the hearing was held. Leonardo was found not guilty; however, the Regidor's signature on the arrest order changed the decision. The Audiencia had never been swifter. Leonardo was sentenced to work in the mines for two years, or pay fifty silver pesos. He had the money, except they would not allow him to return to La Casa Grande. He would be fulfilling the alcalde's sentence in the Mellado Mine, located on the south hill of the city. This mine had a cell for prisoners like Leonardo.

The mine was a stronghold itself. Thick walls surrounded the estate that included a baroque church. After locking the gate and passing the guards, the prisoner was led through a little sidewalk that continued into a granite room. There was a dark well in the middle of a garden just before the room. There was also a patio full of rectangular wooden slots. Women and children stepped on rocks and silver nuggets sprinkled with mercury. They seemed overworked and hungry.

Once inside the building, a locked cell secured coffins of silver pieces. There were men meticulously separating metal and dirt. They were also weighing the precious nuggets. All the miners were peasants. They had a miserable time, and many didn't survive such inhuman conditions. Workers were forced to carry heavy sacks, full of silver and rock, out to the surface. It was terribly dangerous because they had to climb on ladders made of logs with steps that could only fit a little more than the toes. Burning torches were used to light the wall as the miners forced stakes into gaps. The workers lacked protection and equipment in the mines. Many had died due to constant collapses and by having inhaled the underground toxic gases.

Slavery was illegal on paper, but the low wages and abuses were extremely severe.

"You will be here for a long time, until you pay your way out to freedom! Name and place of birth!" a man by the weighing station demanded. He was the task coordinator.

"Leonardo Vallejo, born in La Casa Grande Hacienda at Las Norias, Jalisco," Leonardo replied.

"Vallejo from La Casa Grande, Did you say Vallejo?" the man asked.

"Yes sir. I don't belong here. There has been an injustice! I can pay the fee!" Leonardo disputed now that he had a chance to talk.

"Who's your father?"

"Joaquin Vallejo was my father," answered the cowboy.

"Major Vallejo was your father?"

"Did you know my father?" Leonardo asked.

"Yes, I did. Why are you here? Who signed the order?" The man checked the document and saw Don Julio and the Regidor's name on it. Puzzled, he grabbed his beard and then the back of his head. Joaquin was well known by the mine owners and the soldiers.

He had been a close friend to this man. Nevertheless, he had no choice but to register the young man and put him in the deepest part of the mine. It was a court order. He commanded the guard to take him down the shaft.

"Wait! I told you I could pay! I have the money at La Casa Grande!"

"Why would we do such a foolish thing? We can't let you go! You would not return. If you attempt to leave the mine's perimeter, you will be shot!" the man warned pointing to the guard who pushed Leonardo into the stairs. His hands and feet were untied before he climbed down the steep, deformed stairs.

The heat and lack of oxygen made the shaft a nightmare for the miners. Suddenly, a great commotion startled both men about ten meters down. The guards were pushing a man who apparently had fallen while trying to take the silver out of the mine. He seemed to be crippled by the funny way he walked. He had a heavy sack tied on his back. Since it was heavy to hold, he had lost balance. Leonardo helped him and opened the way to the steps for him to continue to the ground above.

"I guess I will be a miner before I become a doctor." Leonardo said puffing the dust and smoke already hurting his nostrils and eyes.

He was shocked to see young, dusty, skinny boys full of dust. They resembled little skeletons hitting rock with picks.

"So this is how poor peasant boys help out their parents to feed the rest of the family. Just like in the haciendas, the mines are an imprisonment for Mestizos and Indians. It is indeed a tomb for them!" he reasoned, "I will not survive in this hell!"

The Vallejo young man was given a sledgehammer to try his luck on the solid stone. The pain in his arms quickly triggered cramps and a dried cough. Not even the bandana covering his nose and mouth stopped the suffocating dust. After three hours of heavy work, a guard holding a whip called his name. Leonardo was immediately removed from breaking the rock and pushed aside towards one of the logs.

"Get out! The boss needs you on the ground!"

As he climbed up, the stinkiness and the dust felt more tolerable. Shortly after, a slim rush of fresh air welcomed him to the world again. It was a sign that the entrance was near. Leonardo was surprised to see the same man being pushed around. This time he wasn't carrying anything, but he still walking like a turkey. His name was Juan; however, everyone called him Pípila.

Leonardo gained courage when he saw the stars on the sky again, but most of all, he was grateful to breathe clean air again. He was taken to meet with the task coordinator one more time. The man was sitting out in the patio by the well.

"Sit down Vallejo! Bind his feet," the bearded man commanded to a guard holding a musket. "Leave us when you finish!" he then turned to Leonardo, "Look muchacho, I don't know what you did, but I am indebted to your father. You say you have the money to pay the penalty. Where do you have it?"

"Back at La Casa Grande," Leonardo replied.

"Can someone bring it? How can I get it?"

"Only my father and I know where it is? I give you my word that I will come back with the money if you let me go," Leonardo proposed, "send guards with me."

"I'll see what I can do. Tomorrow morning you will be assigned to work on street repairs," the man explained.

"Will you let me bring the coins?" Leonardo asked.

"Not yet, but you should be thankful to be out of the hole! Your father saved my life once, so in exchange, I will change your assignment. From now on, you will spend the nights in the cell next to the silver pesos."

"But I am innocent! I didn't do anything. I need to talk to the Corregidor!" the young man demanded.

"I hope you can recognize your slim opportunity to jump into freedom," the man said without further explanation.

Leonardo was escorted to a room where prisoners were given a ration of bread. He was also given a dark colorful ragged cloth as a blanket. The night was warm but cooled down at dawn.

"A slim opportunity to jump into freedom, what was he talking about? All I know is that I must find a way to escape. Beatriz needs me! I need her so much!"

The following morning, Leonardo was surprised to see his new assignment. He was now part of a group of stonecutters. They were finishing a meter thick wall in a room joining the mine fort and the church building. It was a secret chamber with cruel torturing devices. No one muttered a word, yet their faces resembled the fear they felt every time they saw a coffin with spikes inside the door. There were also hanging cages, racks for splitting the joints, skull repressors and chastity belts. The one that made Leonardo tremble was the guillotine. The smell in the catacomb was so terrible that it caused some men to vomit. Leonardo stood next to a sarcophagus that had sharp spikes on the door. Once it was closed, the spikes became daggers on the human being's chest. The body was then chopped into pieces and burned with mercury acid. The bones were then thrown in a well next to a fire pit.

The crew worked there five hours and then moved outside to build another wall.

At the Regidor's mansion, Beatriz remained locked in a bedroom upstairs. Her family awaited Antonio Vallejo's' arrival from Mexico City. He would bring legal documents to close the La Casa Grande transaction. At the same time, Santiago and three men made the trip back to the stables on the other side of town. He was eager to be back in his racetrack where he usually trained twice a week. He wanted to take a few stallions back to his home stable but was hesitant to bring Beatriz's horse.

Somehow, he resented his first loss to the beast. It was then that someone caught his attention.

"I saw your riders, and I figured that you might be here! I bring luggage for Don Julio and his family. Do you mind if we rest here for a while?" Fermín asked.

"Not at all, come and feed your animals. You might find something to eat inside the storage room next to the windowsill," Santiago replied.

"Do you know if Don Julio inquired about me?" Fermín asked trying to find out how much of his stratagem was known.

"Not that I know. He is organizing the most important ceremony in Guanajuato, my marriage with Beatriz!"

Fermín detested hearing such news; he stared at the bachelor with jealousy and expressed faked best wishes. He turned around and headed straight to the storage room.

After washing himself and sleeping for a while, Fermín went to the corral to check on Santiago. He wanted to know about Don Julio's plans in detail, and about Leonardo's fate.

"Did our common enemy receive his sentence yet?"

"Yes, he did! He was sentenced to hard labor in the Mellado Mine. You know what that means, right?" the bachelor asked.

"Good. He deserves that. Is he really there? We ought to pay him a visit," Fermín suggested.

"Do you think he can run away?" Santiago questioned.

"You never know. It doesn't hurt to check," the ruffian suggested.

"We can do that on our way home." Santiago said.

"Once I deliver my cargo, I will come back and lodge here, unless Don Julio or your father says otherwise," Fermín proposed, "Do you mind?"

"That will be fine. Let's leave for the mine at once. You troubled my mind," Santiago replied.

"Since I will be staying here why don't you take that animal? I hate it with all my guts,"

Fermín said glancing at Lightning.

Santiago smiled and ordered his men to bring the white stallion. It was tied to Fermín's wagon. Both men started their way up the south hill towards the mine. Santiago rode in front followed by two men on the side. Three thoroughbred colts briskly walked between them and the wagon.

Shortly after, they were able to see workers in front of the mine fortress. Leonardo recognized his horse from afar. He turned towards the wall to avoid being recognized as soon as he saw Santiago. Nevertheless, his effort didn't matter because the dust on his face and clothes concealed his identity. Fermín and Santiago left the wagons and the horses outside the mining quarters. They passed the gate and asked for the person in charge.

"I need to see the list of prisoners and registration." Santiago demanded.

He was satisfied to see Leonardo's name and assignment in the mine.

"Great! The law has been respected and served. Go and bring Leonardo Vallejo; we need to confirm his presence," ordered the bachelor.

"With all due respect sir, you need a permit from my superior to interrupt labor," the task coordinator said in a nervous tone.

"I am Santiago del Castillo, son of Regidor Cirilo del Castillo. I don't need anybody's permission to see a prisoner. Go get him yourself immediately!"

The man got up from his seat and went directly to the guard. After whispering in his ear, he turned to Santiago and Fermín and invited them to sit down. Just when they sat, a loud commotion outside the gate caught their attention. One of the horses had gone wild and broke lose. Aware that it was the white stallion, Fermín got up and ran to the street followed by Santiago. Right when they crossed the gate, they saw a miner jump on the white horse and flee the scene.

"IT'S HIM! Quickly! Don't let him get away!" shouted the bachelor.

"I will make sure he doesn't come back!" Fermín replied, jumping on his horse starting the pursuit.

The miners cheered for the young man who was being chased by three men. He hung on to the horse with his knees and hands because his feet were loosely bound. Fermín's men didn't know if they should fire their guns or capture him. Screaming on top of his lungs, Fermín ordered them to fire their weapons, but the distance between them was significant. Santiago couldn't believe his eyes. He fumed running back and forth, then rushed into the fortress and slapped the man in charge.

"I will press charges for negligence and non-compliance!"

He ran outside and stared down the road where the riders disappeared.

"I know you will come back! I know! I will be waiting for you," he said out loud. He then gathered his team and resumed his return home.

A few kilometers away, Leonardo dashed through the canyon. He was ahead of his pursuers by a considerable distance. He knew he would find help in the neighboring towns around the Cubilete Hill. His horse was extremely exhausted, but stopping could be lethal. He found shelter among some tall bushes by a creek. As his animal rested, he tried to break his chains by hitting them with a rock. He ceased once he realized he was making a loud noise.

In Guanajuato, Beatriz was planning her own escape. She was kept in the upper bedroom behind locked doors. She had been told about Leonardo's fate in the mine. Don Julio and the Regidor were downstairs awaiting Antonio's arrival. A telegram for Cirilo was delivered shortly. It came directly from Spain. He immediately opened it and changed his expression once he learned the news. The Duke from Leon had broken his agreement because his daughter had passed away a month ago. That meant no nobility title for his son. Being aware that La Casa Grande transaction would be difficult to be legally granted if Santiago were unmarried, he turned around and addressed Don Julio.

"My son is ready to settle down! He has found the love of his life. He wants to marry your daughter right away!"

The Regidor's new plan was to have the marriage ceremony the next morning and finish the deal in the afternoon. Santiago would legally own the estate and the girl. Don Julio was pleased to hear such good news, so he suggested that his wife and Mrs. Del Castillo should go and bring the family's tailor.

"If he needs to work the whole night he will do so, but my daughter will have the best bride's gown by tomorrow morning," Don Julio said.

Wedding announcements went around the city that afternoon, but only a small circle of friends were invited including the Corregidor. Santiago was pleased to hear the news, so he quickly went to see Beatriz.

"You promised to help Leonardo, and you didn't keep your word," Beatriz claimed.

"I just did! I helped him get away from the mine!" Santiago responded.

"That's a lie! How do I know you are saying the truth?"

"It is true! He fled the city two hours ago. I spoke to the mine coordinator and arranged for his escape. I provided him with your white stallion," Santiago explained, "But you have to understand that he will never come back. He is a fugitive! He is wanted all over the mines. If he is lucky, he will avoid the soldier squads on his way to Jalisco."

"Do you give me your word of honor that you are saying the truth?" the girl begged.

"Of course I am saying the truth! He had to run for his life. You have to understand that a person's life is more valuable than anything in the world. He left forever!"

Beatriz felt a little relief to hear that he was alive. She knew it was just a matter of time, before Leonardo would come for her. Santiago felt her grief and feelings for his rival. Controlling his anger, he took her hand and looked directly into her eyes.

"Beatriz, how can you be so blind? I will make you the happiest woman in the world. I have the means to give you anything you desire. Your father has consented for me to take you as my wife. I would like you to rejoice as much as I do!"

"Santiago, I don't love you! A long time ago, I promised myself that I would only marry the man I loved," Beatriz declared.

"But you also made a promise to me. I have done my part! Your life belongs to me now!"

Enraged by her response, Santiago grabbed her head and kissed her by force.

"I will make you love me! You will become my wife tomorrow at noon!"

"You will not get away with it!" She screamed.

Santiago could not believe that a woman would dare to despise him. He left the room and locked the door behind him. Beatriz was left alone lamenting her misfortune.

"Why can't my parents help me? Why wasn't I involved in this decision?" she wept.

Every minute suffocated her freedom that was sentenced to die the following day.

Meanwhile, outside the town of Silao, a rider cautiously looked back as he advanced parallel to the dirt road. He felt an impulse to stop there, but once he passed the Cubilete Hill, he decided to turn north. He had to travel a few kilometers before he could find the road to Jalisco. He would then go on to La Casa Grande and retrieve the jar with the silver coins.

As he was thus thinking, a deafening sound soared by his shoulder. When he turned back, he saw his enemies firing at him. In seconds, Leonardo rode at full gallop around the hill. Since he was still in chains, the cowboy held on to the horse's hair while clenching with his knees. The high-speed pursuit was witnessed by an orange sun which drew a deformed shadow on the mountain. Meanwhile, Fermín and his men kept on firing at the young man. Leonardo then realized the truth of Mariano's words, "It is impossible to do anything when a rifle's cannon is on your back."

West of the Cubilete elevation, a creek separated two smaller hills. Once in the creek, it was impossible to see the top of the field. Leonardo knew his horse could not go any longer at such rapid pace; therefore, he tried to find a hiding place. At that instant, his colt collapsed without a warning. A bullet had reached his hind thigh. Both, man and beast rolled twice on the dirt. As soon as the cowboy was able to get up, he ran to check on his horse.

"Lightning my friend, I am sorry! Please don't die! Be strong! Don't leave me alone!" Leonardo begged with tears rolling down his face.

A bullet hit millimeters away from him. In a matter of seconds, the men surrounded the cowboy. Fermín immediately, jumped to the ground and grabbed him from the neck. The other men took him to a nearby tree and tied him.

"Say your last prayer because you will soon die! But before I do that take this!" Fermín railed and then punched him. "You almost spoiled my plans and caused my ruin! But you won't get on my way anymore! A new order has begun! I call the shots now. You will join your father in hell! He also got in my way, and I had to eliminate him."

"You dirty rat! So you assassinated my father!" Leonardo cried.

"He was a brown noser. He wouldn't let me take the silver to aid the insurgent movement. And do you know why he did it? He wanted to become General Allende's favorite ally. He wanted to move up and then seize control. I couldn't allow a Spaniard to be at the top of the new order."

"You are a traitor! You have no honor or dignity! You will not get away with it!" Leonardo disputed.

"No one can stop me now! No one!" Fermín howled slapping the young man again.

As he was doing so, two riders approached the site. Fermín's men turned and quickly aimed their weapons at them; however, the riders also pointed their guns at them. They appeared to be two soldier scouts from the insurgent army.

"What is going on here?"

"This is none of your business. Get out of here!" Fermín demanded.

"Leave the man alone, and give up your weapons!" the soldiers ordered.

Thinking that they were in control, Fermín's men fired their weapons missing their target. They were shot a second later by the soldiers. Fermín began to tremble and to ask for mercy.

"DON'T SHOOT! PLEASE DON'T SHOOT! I don't want to die!" he said throwing away his gun. "Let me explain! This man is a fugitive! He attempted to murder Don Julio Cortez and abducted his daughter! He was sentenced to work in the mines. I have captured him, and I was going to bring him back to justice."

"Who commissioned you to arrest this man? Who is your superior?" the revolutionary soldiers demanded.

"Don Julio Cortez, the Cieneguilla Hacendado," responded Fermín.

However, after realizing that he had given the wrong answer, he objected saying,

"No, my real boss is General Ignacio Allende! I work for him!"

"General Allende is aware of this fugitive?" inquired the insurgents.

Fermín remained silent.

"Answer the question! Did General Allende order you to arrest this man?"

Just when he was about to answer, an uncountable multitude became visible on top of the hill.

Their voices were like rolling thunder, and their torches illuminated their resolute faces. It was the biggest army assembled in the land. Fermín was amazed and didn't know what it meant. The army mob seemed to be led by a priest who was riding a white stallion; his face projected assurance and determination. He was Miguel Hidalgo, the priest from Dolores, writing freedom with the sword of justice and carving his name in the heart of history. As he got closer, he lifted his hand to stop the advancement, and motioned to his men to investigate the matter. The soldiers proceeded, pushing Fermín towards the crowd, and releasing Leonardo. When the man on the horse saw Leonardo's chains, he was furious and immediately ordered his men to break them. He was a man who despised tyranny, injustice, and slavery. He turned to Fermín and interrogated him.

"What's your name and who do you work for?" the leader demanded.

"My name is Fermín Rodriguez. I am Don Julio Cortez's right hand and administrator at the Cieneguilla Hacienda. This man is a traitor! He betrayed the Hacendado, and he took his daughter! He belongs in jail!" Fermín assured.

The leader turned to the young man trying to read his face, "Are you a Realist?"

"No, I want equal rights for peasants," Leonardo answered, "This rat of a man assassinated my father, Joaquin Vallejo."

"What do you want to do with him?" the commander said pointing to a trembling Fermín.

"This man is a tyrant!" Leonardo said kicking Fermín right where it hurts the most.

"Don Julio Cortez, the Cieneguilla Hacendado betrayed me. He has imprisoned his daughter in Guanajuato to keep us apart."

"Go get her! We will come after you!" the priest leader said pointing to Leonardo's horse.

The colt had rested a little and was up and walking. The bullet that had reached him only made a scratch at the same time the animal tripped.

While insurgents continued to march, Leonardo noticed Hidalgo lifting a banner. It was a symbol of unity and identity. The young man mounted his horse and left the scene.

"IGUALDAD, JUSTICIA, y LIBERTAD!" the priest shouted leading the army on. Everything happened so rapidly that Fermín could not run away from their path. Consequently, the angry mob and their horses trampled him. The life of the tyrant ended without a sign and without a trace. His body remained on the open field only to be devoured by scavengers.

Leonardo rode straight to the town of Silao. The town had been sacked and robbed by insurgents; inevitably, most of its citizens had fled to Guanajuato seeking refuge. The cowboy finally found refuge in an abandoned house. After securing Lightning, he collapsed from exhaustion in the middle of the room. He slept through the whole night. Not even the noise of the mob and the bullets disturbed his sleep.

The following morning, he couldn't remember where he was. Scared, he ran out of the house thinking he was in the mine's hole. After recollecting the events of the previous day, he remembered Beatriz and his promise to help her. Anxiously, he looked around the house for alternatives, immediately he detected a steel, sharp sword hanging on the wall. He also found clean clothes in one of the chambers and went outside to wash himself. Securing the sword to his waist, he decided it was time to stand and reconquer what he had lost.

At the Regidor's house, Don Julio was excited to see his old friend Antonio Vallejo. They were satisfied on how things had worked out for their own benefit.

"So what did you do with the heathen?" Antonio asked.

"He is working in the mines," Don Julio replied with a sarcastic laugh.

"You are slick! You will take half of La Casa Grande and become part of the Regidor's family! You are indeed an astute man!" Antonio taunted.

"You are a good salesman," Don Julio said, "Maybe the Regidor will award you with your brother's medal."

"I deserve a medal; I blew the whistle on the rebel conspiracy. Their secret movement was discovered in Queretaro. If they succeed in overthrowing the government, they plan to take away the land and grant it to the peasants! I had to warn General Callejas for protection. He already mobilized the entire army. Even the Vice-Royalty is aware. You know what that means?" Antonio asked.

"Are you saying that you denounced the whole secret movement?" Don Julio inquired.

"Yes, but we are clean. They will never find out we were part of it."

"Of course, we are one hundred percent Realists," Don Julio declared.

"That's right my friend, and with this wedding you almost become part of Royalty!"

Antonio smiled and then asked in a serious tone, "Where is the silver? I know Fermín and your men took it."

"Which silver? What are you talking about?" the Hacendado questioned.

"Joaquin's army was escorting three coffins of gold and silver. Sergeant Portillo told me that you hid it well."

"I am not aware. I didn't know there was silver involved. I never ordered Fermín anything!

Wait a minute! Was Fermín there at the river?" Don Julio asked.

"Are you sure you don't know?" Antonio questioned.

"No. I am in the dark. Tell me what you know!" Don Julio demanded.

"Fermín took over the operation. He intercepted the cargo before it reached Allende's army. The silver was divided. Fermín took one container and Portillo took another. The third one went to you. Where is it?" Antonio insisted.

"It's all new to me. I never received anything! I wasn't aware," Don Julio explained.

"We are in deep trouble! Fermín or Portillo is behind it! They can blow the whole thing off! Do you know what that means? We must find them at once!" Antonio whispered with distress.

Don Julio began to realize that Leonardo and Beatriz were saying the truth about Fermín. He had no choice than to play along until he met with Fermín.

"Gentleman, the recorder is here; let's all go into my private office to finalize the transaction," the Regidor interrupted.

The four men entered a room full of bookshelves and swords on display cases. At the end of the room, there were silver horse statues on a brown desk. Don Julio and Antonio felt tense but tried to hide their anxiety. The Regidor would turn them in if he knew they had ties with rebel forces.

"If everyone can sign here we would then only need Santiago Del Castillo's signature accepting ownership of La Casa Grande," the city's registrar explained. "He needs to be a married man!"

"He is! He is!" the Regidor assured looking at Don Julio, "It is just a matter of minutes."

He rang a bell, and commanded a maid to call Santiago to come downstairs. When Santiago showed up, he was dressed in his wedding attire. He took the pen and signed his name on the document, making him the sole owner of La Casa Grande Hacienda.

At that instant, a loud knock at the door interrupted the celebration. It was a soldier sent from Corregidor Reaño. He had terrible news.

"The insurgent army has been spotted on its way to Guanajuato. The Spanish army led by Commander Calleja is away from town and thus unable to resist revolutionaries. We must find safety at the Alhóndiga fortress!" The Regidor advised trying to contain his anxiety.

"I will not have my wedding spoiled by heathen peasants and dirty miners!" Santiago uttered,
"Father we must proceed at once!"
"Yes. If you don't mind recording my son's marriage while I will send for the priest," Cirilo del Castillo said turning to the registrar.
"And I will make sure the bride is ready," Don Julio said.
Don Julio hurried upstairs and unlocked Beatriz's door. When he entered the room and saw his daughter holding her beautiful, white, and silver gown, he was filled with emotion.
"You will look lovely!" he said, "Today should be the happiest day of your life. Change that face!"
"Father, you should know that I love Leonardo with all my heart, and I wish it was him whom I was marrying!" Beatriz declared, releasing a heavy sigh from her chest.
"Are you out of your mind? Don't you dare say that in front of Santiago!"
"He already knows. He agreed to let Leonardo go free if I became his wife," the girl affirmed.
"What are you saying? Santiago would never do such a foolish thing! If he did, he did it because he loves you. Make your best effort to deserve his love, or you will not be happy!" Don Julio commanded.
"Father, you don't care about my happiness. You only care about yourself, and your idea of happiness is unreal. You will find out that riches and position are worthless if the main element is missing in life. Happiness is being free to choose who you love and respect. Someday, you will regret making my life miserable!" Beatriz lamented.
Don Julio looked intensely at his daughter. For the first time he felt guilty about his desires.
Ahead of the insurgent army, a lonely rider trotted through the narrow Guanajuato streets. The air felt heavy

to breathe and the sky turned gray. Leonardo asked twice for directions to the Regidor's house but no one paid attention to him. The people were fleeing or locking their homes. He continued east all the way to the San Diego Church. He then spotted a priest and some servants on their way to the Regidor's mansion. They quickly pointed to the house where the soldiers roamed. Leonardo went to the south side avoiding the soldiers. He stopped by the fountain and then continued into the narrow alley below the balconies.

Inside the mansion, Beatriz refused to put on the wedding gown. Even though she had given Santiago her word, she could not do it. Her parents were worried about her disposition. They encouraged her, trying to help her realize the benefits of marrying Santiago Del Castillo. Slowly, fighting against her desire, she finally consented to put on the dress.

Reluctantly, she agreed to come to the living room where everyone waited. When she exited her chamber, she looked straight across into the opposite bedroom. Two open French doors with flowing curtains tempted her to run off. As she walked down the stairs, everyone's eyes were focused on her. The guests were astonished when they saw the bride. She resembled an angelical princess full of charm and splendor. The very sea pearls would be ashamed to rival such a beauty. Before seeing Santiago, an urgent impression rushed her mind to go back to the room.

"Wait! I need to look at myself in the mirror one last time; I will be back in a minute. Mother can you come with me?" Beatriz whispered.

"Don't make us wait long," Don Julio warned.

Mrs. Cortez and Beatriz returned to the room and left the door wide open. The mirror was on the wall opposite the door. She looked at herself and beyond her reflection; she saw an open room with a balcony at the end. A familiar persona became visible on the mirror. She quickly turned around and discovered Leonardo on the opposing balcony. Surprised, she did not know what to say. She thought it was her imagination. Suddenly, the fugitive invited her to come quietly. Beatriz ran out the chamber closing the door behind her. She did not give her mother a chance to follow her. She also locked the door, after she entered the second room. Leonardo impatiently waited on the neighbor's balcony across the alley. The adjacent house was unoccupied because the owners had fled to the Alhondiga. Leonardo and Beatriz stood facing each other a meter apart in opposite balconies. The young man held on to the metal bars and extended his hand to hold Beatriz. She was thrilled to see him but afraid to be discovered. Mrs. Cortez' cries made everyone run upstairs only to be stopped by a locked door.

"Hurry Beatriz, we don't have much time!" Leonardo cried from the other side.

"I knew you would come for me! I knew it!" the girl said, "But I can't jump that far!"

"You have to do it! You have no choice. Come on, trust me. I will catch you!"

The young woman looked around trying to find another alternative. She finally climbed over the balcony's edge and closed her eyes.

"You must fly! Do not be afraid. Believe; you can do it!" Leonardo encouraged extending his arms.

When Beatriz heard the uproar behind her, she finally gained courage to jump to the other balcony. Leonardo with two strong arms pulled her over the edge. A serene, love-reassuring embrace engulfed the two lovers.

"I thought I had lost you!" he said as he cleaned her tears. Beatriz could not explain her joy. It was their moment in time and history. A young bride in love with a lone cowboy, right there in an alley, right in the middle of a city in chaos, battling society's unfair caste system, and running from imposing parents. The couple stood in a balcony that held their feelings and dreams. Leonardo was with his back to the Regidor's house as he kissed her tender lips.

The door was broken down, and an irate Hacendado ran to the balcony. As soon as he saw his daughter in the fugitive's arms, he took a sharp sword from the wall and charged at them. Everything happened so fast that Leonardo could not realize the danger. When Beatriz noticed her Don Julio advancing from the opposite balcony, she pushed Leonardo aside to prevent her father from stabbing him in the back. Leonardo was truly the love of her life, and she had traded her life for his. In an instant, her beautiful white dress was covered in blood. Don Julio couldn't believe what he had done.

"No! Beatriz! My daughter! I didn't mean to...!" He cried, "You! It is all your fault!"

The helpless father pointed the sword at the cowboy and threw it, but he missed by a couple feet. On the street, the mob had assembled and began to ransack the neighborhood.

"Beatriz, my love, don't leave me! Don't leave me alone. Don't do this now!" Leonardo cried.

With an agonizing voice, the young woman repeated his name, and lay drained from the wound.

"Leonardo, Leonardo, you came back for me! You are here, and that is all that matters! Your love endures strong in my heart!" The young man was desperate but not because he was surrounded by the mob.

"I will never leave you! I will take you with me! Please look at me, stay strong for us, and for our love," the sobbing cowboy begged.

"Leonardo, I finally feel free! I love you! Don't cry for me: my love is stronger than my pain. I can see my freedom! I can see my freedom!" Beatriz whispered in agony.

"BEATRIZ! BEATRIZ! MY DAUGHTER IS DYING! GET A DOCTOR! PLEASE!" Mrs. Cortez pleaded with anyone who would sympathize with her grief.

The men in the Regidor's house ran downstairs determined to eliminate Leonardo. They were about to step a foot out of the front door, when the mob tried to break in the house. The Regidor quickly handed a pistol to the men in the house, and commanded everyone to board the stage wagon at the back of his house. Ten soldiers guarded the stagecoach. Don Julio had to forcefully drag his crying wife to the carriage as she called for her daughter. They could only find safety at the Alhóndiga fortress.

"Santiago and his men will bring her! Get in the cart!" shouted Don Julio as he opened the door.

"I NEED TO SEE MY DAUGHTER! SHE NEEDS ME!" Mrs. Cortez yelled resisting her husband's effort.

"Your daughter chose to leave us! She put herself in such a perilous situation! Santiago is risking his own life to save her. Let me go and help him!" Don Julio explained pushing her into the carriage. He then ran back to the house for the last time. The Hacendado was determined to take care of Leonardo once and for all. With a pistol in his right hand, he crossed the main entrance to the street. The scene was horrific! He had to avoid stepping on the deceased and the wounded. The ununiformed corpses were an indication that Santiago and the soldiers had prevailed.

Meanwhile, Santiago and five soldiers made way through the crowd into the empty house. Santiago was upstairs trying to take Beatriz from Leonardo's arms. The struggle began. They wrestled on the floor ignoring Beatriz.

"We need a doctor! There is no time for fighting! Find a doctor!" Leonardo insisted.

"You tried to steal my bride twice. I will make sure it doesn't happen again!" Santiago howled in a threatening tone.

"She is not your bride, and I didn't steal her! She willingly chose to come with me!"

Leonardo responded.

As they wrestled, the house erupted in flames on the first floor. Leonardo beat him at every punch cornering him by the wall. Pushing a bookcase, Santiago temporarily knocked Leonardo out. He then took Beatriz and rushed downstairs calling out loud for help. On his way outside, the bachelor found Don Julio who took his daughter from his arms.

"My sweet girl! Why did you get in the way?" he lamented. Both rushed into the Regidor's house.

"Hurry! They are waiting for us in the back!" Don Julio screamed while Santiago pushed a broken door.

"I need to tend to her wound immediately! She is not going to make it!" Santiago cried, "Let me bring my medicine tools."

"If you truly love her you will heal her! Come on! Use what they taught you in medicine school! Prove to me that you deserve her love!" the Hacendado demanded.

"I will start once we get in the carriage, but first, let me look at her wound more carefully!"

Inside the house, Leonardo finally came to his senses and got up. He ran downstairs trying to get out; however, it was impossible for him to go through the flames. He then ran to the balcony, which was his only escape route. Noticing that the city was in turmoil, the Vallejo young man jumped into the Regidor's balcony. He ran across the chamber towards the main floor. The cowboy checked and called everywhere before coming through the back door. He then was able to see the wagon, already on the street, on its way to the fortress. He knew it was them because the guards followed closely. Taking one of the stallions, he fled downtown being careful not to be mistaken for a Realist. At a considerable distance, a violent mob viciously advanced to the Alhondiga granary too.

The stagecoach was attacked but the escorting guards' relentless firing deterred anyone from coming close to the vehicle. The sticks and stones on the street proved to be a risk. Many times the buggy almost tipped over. The rider behind dashed like a flash in the middle of danger. Not even the guards' bullets discouraged his intention.

"I need to stop them before they enter the fort," Leonardo thought as he galloped through the debris on the road. "Beatriz is dying, and she is being taken to the wrong side of the battle. The city is lost in chaos! No one will help me and I don't have weapons or power to stop the crowd."

He looked to heaven begging for divine intervention and then to the sides. When he looked straight again, he had already lost sight of his target. He then turned to the left and felt relieved to see the fleeing carriage again. The vehicle finally came to a stop at the north entrance of the unyielding structure.

The Alhóndiga

Led by the charismatic priest Miguel Hidalgo y Costilla, the revolutionaries invaded the city of Guanajuato, only to find that the Spanish had all sought refuge in the Alhóndiga de Granaditas, the town's granary. It was here that Don Julio, Antonio, the Regidor, and his followers would hide like scared foxes.

Made of impenetrable stone, the Alhóndiga was a virtual fortress offering the Spanish protection and an offensive position to shoot at anyone approaching them. Several firing squads were guarding the north door when the Regidor's stagecoach approached the entrance. The soldiers, mine owners, rich creoles, politicians, and their families made up a group of about five hundred aristocrats who sought refuge at the granary. Both heavy, mesquite, wooden doors were secured and became impossible to penetrate. Realists waited, hoping for some reinforcements from the capital or some other post. It was a symbolic description of the country. The few hundred inside held all the wealth and power as the thousands of peasants struggled for freedom and bread outside.

Leonardo mingled among the peasants whose rocks became weak missiles only marking the thick stone walls. He never caught up with Beatriz, but his spirit was stronger than the granite fortification and the vicious lead balls. His sadness became anger, and his anger became sadness. His life did not have a purpose now that Beatriz was gone.

"How can I stop this sea of men from hurting Beatriz," he thought.

He had two reasons to break into the fort, so he joined the struggle for independence with greater determination. He placed himself in the front line.

The Insurgents were desperate. The building seemed to be impenetrable. Many men were falling as they tried to approach the two doors or climb the walls. Besides, Realist reinforcements could be approaching anytime. Hidalgo and the other officials concluded that their only hope for victory was to destroy one of the doors to enter the premises; but who would do it? Who would dare to approach the door, dodge bullets, and set it on fire? No one was willing to take such a life threatening risk, until El Pipila appeared from among the peasants. The very miner who was pushed around at the mine was filled with hatred in his chest and thirst for revenge against the mine owners. He approached Hidalgo and volunteered to burn the door. As they pondered how to do it, el Pipila remembered the many times he had carried beams and slate stones on his back in and out of the mines. The idea quickly began to burn in his head. He rapidly found a piece of thick stone and asked his friends to fastened it on his back. It would be his protection against bullets while he crawled to the door. When Leonardo recognized his friend, he quickly ran to help. Once ready, Juan Jose el Pipila began to crawl under enemy fire. The stone was almost impossible to bear, but his pride and determination for freedom gave him the courage and strength to continue. The insurgents charged with encouragement when he finally reached the entrance. Immediately after setting fire to the wooden door, the Insurgent Army swarmed the building like vultures on carcasses.

"Please, I beg you! My bride is in there! Spare her life! She was taken captive! She is one of us!"

The scene was terrifying. As soon as the door caught on fire, the natives launched to attack. Leonardo was helpless; his efforts to save Beatriz had been vain. No one stopped to pay attention to him.

The Spanish soldiers fired all their ammunition on the first rebels who came in; however, it was impossible to hold them all. Inside the Alhóndiga, everyone including women and children were massacred by the mob.

Leonardo ran to the jail, the most secured spot in the building. He first identified the Regidor's body and then the women. He was astonished to see the mob taking Antonio's coat and belongings. He searched every dead body trying to find Beatriz. In the corner of the dungeon, he discovered that someone was alive. With a deep wound on his chest, Don Julio laid on the ground.

"She didn't come! Go find her, you have my blessing!" the Hacendado said before his last breath. Insurgents had their first victory as they took the Alhondiga.

Leonardo rushed back to the Regidor's house while the city was being looted. As he ran in the street, his legs felt heavy and his lungs screamed for oxygen. He realized that Santiago had stayed behind with Beatriz. The city was in turmoil; every house and business around him was being plundered.

"Oh heavens, please! Let me find her again!" he cried.

He rested against a wall to catch his breath for a few seconds, and then continued all the way until he reached the fountain in front of the house. Realizing that it was impossible to enter the house through the front, he went around it and entered through the back door. Leonardo was happy to see his white stallion in the corral.

"Where were you when I needed you most?" he claimed as he passed by the horse.

When he entered the house, he desperately called for Beatriz hoping to hear a response. A loud noise in the office enticed him to follow in that direction. Moving like a jaguar in the bushes, he entered the office when unexpectedly, a bullet struck him in the shoulder. Luckily it was only an abrasion. An irate Santiago prepared to fire again.

"You never give up! But this will be the end of your stubbornness!" shouted the bachelor.

As the cowboy lay on the floor, Santiago pointed his gun at his face. After realizing that the pistol did not have gun powder, he rushed to take his sword from its case to charge against Leonardo. His action gave the cowboy enough time to jump on his feet and pull out his sword.

"Where is she? I would be willing to die if she is gone!" Leonardo shouted avoiding a stab.

"You deserve to die anyway!" replied the bachelor.

"This struggle is for her and for my freedom! My ancestors deserve it!" the cowboy cried pushing away from a clinch and dodging a punch.

"I will have her love! My class will crush traitors to the Crown like you! Your kind only live to serve and be led," Santiago muttered gnashing his teeth.

"Beatriz chose me! She chose me!" Leonardo taunted, "Not even all your riches and your arrogance could prove your pretended superiority!"

They charged and blocked swings as the cowboy leaned against the back door. He knew that the smallest mistake could cost him his life. Leonardo was no match for the bachelor. With a nimble movement, Santiago disarmed the young man. The Regidor's son only needed a tenth of a second to deliver the final blow, but before he did it, he wanted to humiliate the cowboy.

"Before I kill you, I want to prove why Beatriz is better by my side. I am a doctor! For years, I trained my mind and my hands for tragedies like this one. Don't you understand that I saved her for me? She needs my care to recover from her mortal wound. She needs me now! You are a servant! What will you do for her? She will die by your side! That's why I am the better man. I was born a better man! This is my destiny, and this is yours! Say good bye to the world!"

Just then someone fired through a window and struck the bachelor on his leg dropping him to the floor. Realizing that someone had broken into the mansion, the cowboy swiftly crawled under a nearby desk for protection. He stayed there for a second, hearing the intruder approaching his side of the room. The steps on the floor presaged the imminent threat. He waited for a second, holding a sword tightly on his right hand, he was prepared to surprise the intruder. All of a sudden, a soft voice caught his attention.

"Leonardo!"

It was the voice of the one who had traded her life for his, the voice of the girl he loved appeasing his anxiety and restoring his peace. There she was with a musket, leaning against the desk. Leonardo quickly got up and passed over the wounded bachelor. When he saw Beatriz alive, he was overwhelmed with joy.

"Beatriz! My love!"

"Leonardo!" She answered before falling in his arms exhausted.

"My life has no purpose without you, I love you!" she whispered.

"Don't say more, I will take you with me this time," Leonardo replied.

Beatriz not only survived her wound because Santiago gave her quick medical attention, but because her will to be with the one she loved was stronger.

Leonardo quickly carried her outside the house; however, he felt impressed to close the previous argument Santiago had started.

"I am grateful for what you did for Beatriz, but do not be mistaken; she is not alive because of you. Her love was deeper than her wound. She lived to be with me. Today, I am the better man! Our love has surpassed that which for many of you was unreasonable. Fate joined us, and now fate will lead us together!"

Outside the mansion, the mob had set the door on fire in order to break in. Leonardo took Beatriz to the back door and put her on his horse. He tried to go back for Santiago, but he was nowhere to be found. The bachelor had trapped himself in a secret chamber in the basement as the property was consumed by the flames. The two riders rapidly fled the scene hoping to nurture their love and their freedom.

From the northwest hill, Beatriz and Leonardo were able to see the city burn. It was the first real battle for freedom, freedom to choose, freedom to love, and freedom to realize dreams. With the sunset on their backs, the young couple were ready to start their new lives together.

It was a new era; a new country was being born. A new government would take over New Spain. Freedom had been so close to death. Only time, justice, and equality could heal its wounds.

Leonardo and Beatriz headed north stopping to see the priest in Teochaltiche and then to La Casa Grande. After they recuperated from their physical and emotional injuries, they continued north to a peaceful land full of opportunities. As they reflected on their tribulations and their journey together, they recognized an invisible hand leading them to safety. It was the voice and desire of those who had gone before them, crying to their Creator on their behalf.

Near the Corona del Mar beach in Alta California, a white stallion roamed through the shores. A young couple sat on the sand watching the immense orange sun sink into the blue sea. The San Joaquin Hills filled with orange trees accompanied their peaceful stay, and the Santa Ana winds were only a whisper of old Mexico. Freedom never died, but it remained wounded according to the mandates of those in power.

Bibliography

1. Sosa, Francisco (1985). *Biografias de Mexicanos Distinguidos-Miguel Hidalgo* (in Spanish) 472. Mexico City: Editorial Porrua SA. pp. 288–92. ISBN 968-452-050-6.

2. Part II: Miguel Hidalgo y Costilla (1753–1811)" (in Spanish). Retrieved 27 November 2008

3. Vazquez-Gomez, Juana (1997). Westport, Connecticut: Greenwood Publishing Group, Incorporated. ISBN 978-0-313-30049-3.

4. Tuck, Jim. "Miguel Hidalgo: The Father Who Fathered a Country (1753–1811)". Retrieved 27 November 2008.

5. Wikipedia.org